A WOMAN
OF HER TRIBE

A WOMAN
OF HER TRIBE

◇ ◇ ◇

MARGARET A. ROBINSON

CHARLES SCRIBNER'S SONS • NEW YORK
Collier Macmillan Canada • Toronto
Maxwell Macmillan International Publishing Group
New York • Oxford • Hong Kong • Singapore • Sydney

Charles Scribner's Sons Books for Young Readers
Macmillan Publishing Company
866 Third Avenue, New York, NY 10022
Collier Macmillan Canada, Inc.
1200 Eglinton Avenue East, Suite 200
Don Mills, Ontario M3C 3N1

First Edition   10 9 8 7 6 5 4 3 2 1
Printed in the United States of America

Library of Congress Cataloging-in-Publication Data
Robinson, Margaret A.
A woman of her tribe / Margaret A. Robinson.—1st ed.   p.   cm.
Summary: Fifteen-year-old Annette, whose dead father was a Nootka Indian, travels with her English mother from their country home on Vancouver Island to the city of Victoria and seeks to find her own way in deciding which cultural heritage she should pursue.
[1. Nootka Indians—Fiction.
2. Indians of North America—British Columbia—Fiction.
3. Vancouver Island (B.C.)—Fiction.]   I. Title.
PZ7.R56744Wo 1990   [Fic]—dc20   90-31534   CIP   AC
ISBN 0-684-19223-3

For Zoe and Toby

The author wishes to acknowledge her indebtedness to *Daughters of Copper Woman* by Anne Cameron. And to say thank you to Seiko Marton.

A WOMAN
OF HER TRIBE

◊ 1 ◊

Annette started up the logging road, walking barefoot in the warm September sun. She wanted to take a last look at the eagles' nest at the top of the headland above the beach. Sea goldenrod studded the steep dirt track with bursts of yellow, next to everlasting, white and starry. A salt breeze cooled her back. Insects buzzed and a gull called.

The old pine holding the nest stood fierce and solitary near the clifftop. The other trees grew in a grove down the slope, out of the wind. The young birds had grown big enough to leave the nest long ago. She'd watched the parents feed the raucous nestlings and seen one of the fledglings launch out, beating his untried wings against the insubstantial air.

She scanned the sky on the chance of seeing a quick, dark mark against the gauzy blue, but though a gull floated on an updraft, there were no eagles. She moved to the edge of the grove and sat in her usual spot, smelling

1

resin, leaning against a pine's bark, against its hard, rough skin. She listened to the distant sound of the surf. As she gazed at a small purple aster growing near her hand, time slowed almost to a stop. Then a flock of sandpipers, wheeling and calling above the cliff, announced an arrival.

Florence, Annette's best friend, stood above her, blocking the sun: strong bare legs in cutoffs, faded T-shirt over small breasts and broad shoulders, broad Nootka face. Annette's father had been a full-blooded Nootka.

"Your mum says the car's all packed."

Her message delivered, Florence sat on the ground where she had stood. Her back was still to the sun, but Annette could see her eyes now, dark, quiet, and unhurried but also a little sad. Annette was grateful for her company. Silently, she said good-bye to the eagles' nest and the pine grove. When she was finished, they stood up and walked to the logging road. As though at a common signal, they broke into an easy run, barely faster than a walk. Florence's thick black braid bounced on her back. Dust puffs rose around their bare feet as they beat out a mutual rhythm. Annette wondered when she and Florence would run together again.

They took the slope back down to the beach in bigger, faster steps. The hill lent its power, putting a hand on their backs. At the bottom, Annette bent at the water's edge, scooped up a handful, and sucked it up with her lips. Cold, wet, strong, saltier than blood. She swished it over her teeth and spat it onto the sand.

"Everyone's there to see you off," said Florence.

"Kiki, too?"

"Sure—the third musketeer. And Gino. He didn't take the boat out today, even though the salmon are starting to run."

"Ah," said Annette. Gino was Florence's stepfather. By taking the day off, he was honoring Mum, who had delivered his babies.

Florence dug her feet into the damp sand and let the sea-foam wash them. Annette did the same. Standing on their edge of Vancouver Island, they looked across the wide expanse of water, glassy green nearby, then blue, then gray where it melted into the horizon. Somewhere over there, Annette thought, are the Aleutians and Russia. To the south, Japan.

"This is for you," Florence said.

From her pocket she pulled a red knee sock, threadbare in the sole. It had a small hole in the toe and another in the heel. Since neither home had a phone, it was their signal, between Granmaw's trailer, where Annette often stayed when her mum went on her nursing trips up the coast, and Florence's house. If Annette looked out her bedroom window and saw the sock in Florence's window, it meant "Come." Annette used the sock's mate as a similar signal.

Annette looked at Florence and smiled. When Florence smiled her slow smile in return, Annette took a blue envelope from her pocket and handed it to her.

Florence read the blue sheet of stationery Annette had put inside and on which she'd written her new Victoria address.

"There's a box of envelopes and paper," said Annette. "A little hint. I left it on the shelf over your bed, up high where the babies can't get it." Florence shared her bedroom with her toddler half brother and baby half sister. Her mother baby-sat other little kids, too. Nothing was safe at Florence's house.

"I'm not much of a letter writer," Florence said. She

folded the note carefully, thrust it deep into the pocket of her cutoffs, and patted the pocket once.

"Neither am I." Annette rolled the sock and tucked it deep into the pocket of the new cotton pants Mum had bought her for the trip.

The water was swirling cold around their ankles, sinking their heels into the sand, leaving their toes high. Annette didn't want to leave, but finally they pulled their feet out and washed the sand off them. Slowly, they ran up the beach, past the boats and dock, and past the school they had both attended for ten years. Florence had been scared of the teacher on the first day. She hadn't been around many strangers, especially new white people. She didn't cry. She just froze outside the school and couldn't move. Annette had taken Florence's hand. They had walked up the steps and into the schoolroom together.

Now, bare feet landing lightly, they ran down the dirt road that wound through the woods, past Granmaw's trailer, past Florence's house, and finally to the village, where Annette and Mum had lived in the apartment above the clinic. The bleached gray shingles of the small building looked peaceful.

"We're all set to go," Mum called. Slender and blonde, she was dressed up in a denim skirt instead of jeans but wore her usual plaid shirt with the sleeves rolled up. She was unfolding a map next to the secondhand car she'd bought. Gino had been tinkering with it to get it in shape for the road. Till now, she'd always used a beat-up government jeep.

The car was stuffed. The roof rack was loaded and the backseat was filled right up to the ceiling.

Mum spread a street map of Victoria out over the hood. "That's where we'll be living." She pointed. "That's the

4

hospital where I'll be working. And that's St. John's, Annette's new school. I just know I'm going to get lost. Can you see me driving in all that traffic?"

Kiki towered over Mum, peering at the map over her shoulder. On that first day of school he'd been smaller than Annette, even though he was a year older, sixteen now. Annette, no matter how much she ate, stayed small, flat chested, and thin. Sometimes she felt left out, as though Florence and Kiki were turning into grown-ups without her. "These things are genetically timed," Mum had told her, offering small comfort. "You take after me."

Gino paid no attention to the map. On this part of the island, he could find his way anywhere on land or water without a piece of paper covered with a maze of lines and squares. He seemed uneasy, the way he was anywhere except on his boat or in his workshop. Florence's mother, Vera, had Tom in a carrier on her back, and the baby, Wilma, in her arms. Vera's usual cigarette was tucked deep in the corner of her mouth. The eye above the cigarette squinted against the smoke.

Mary Jones, Granmaw's friend and old like Granmaw, was too Nootka to have any faith in maps. She and Granmaw sat on the clinic steps like stumps in the sun. Annette didn't want to look at the map right now. Mum had said she was counting on Annette to navigate, but first there would be hours and hours of highway. She'd see the city soon enough. Right now she wanted to fill her eyes with the people around her. She went and sat between Granmaw and Mary.

Mum was hugging and kissing everyone good-bye. Then she ran back into the apartment. "I have to go to the bathroom one more time," she said, laughing.

Annette leaned over and hugged Mary Jones. She

5

leaned over and hugged Granmaw. They would not look at her and they were not huggers, but she could tell that they were pleased. When Annette stood up, Vera threw away her cigarette and kissed her cheek across the baby's head. "Stay out of trouble down there," she said. "Don't forget us."

"I could never do that," said Annette.

Gino smiled and nodded. Kiki, looking awkward, shook her hand. Florence's hug was hard and fast; Annette hugged her back the same way. She could feel the rolled-up sock, a lump in her pocket, pressed between them.

"I'll write first," Annette said. Then she got into the car.

"Wouldn't it be awful if it wouldn't start," Mum said out the window to Gino, but the engine caught. Gino's eyes crinkled with satisfaction. Mum drove the overloaded vehicle slowly down the road. It seemed to heave itself through the ruts like a boat cresting and dipping over waves. Mum glanced in the rearview mirror and fluttered her hand out her window. Annette stuck her head out her window and waved good-bye. Florence, Kiki, and Vera waved back. Granmaw had moved off the steps and stood in the road apart from the others, watching the car leave. Annette kept her eyes on Granmaw till the road curved and she was gone from sight.

"They were awfully nice," Mum said, "considering they think I'm crazy."

"Florence and Kiki don't think that."

"But Granmaw does, and Mary, and Gino, and Vera. They think your father wouldn't like it, my taking you away."

Annette said nothing. Her father had died in Vietnam when she was a baby. She had only a few memories of him. Or maybe they were dreams. Or stories she had made up to go with the photographs Mum had given her.

Mum squared her shoulders in a way Annette had seen many times, before she gave shots. She didn't like hurting people, but she'd told Annette that the best way was to "just get on with it."

"Your father's not here to ask," Mum said, looking straight down the road. "You were smart enough to get that scholarship. And I was lucky enough to get a job. So."

Annette finished the sentence for Mum. "So, we can't do anything but give it a try." She'd never been away from Port West. She'd heard that Indian kids had a hard time when they tried to make it in white Victoria schools. She smoothed a wrinkle in the new cotton pants.

"Oh, Annette," Mum said. "I'm lucky to have you." Her glance started warmly with Annette's face and ended coolly with her feet. "Where's your shoes?" she asked.

"In the backseat, of course," said Annette. "I'm fifteen—remember? You're going to have to stop asking me stuff like that."

◊ 2 ◊

Annette yawned and stretched as they waited at a red light. Laura's Gifts, on their right, displayed boxes of toffee and jars of jam. The boxes and jars had little British Columbia flags sticking up from them. On the other side, in The English Tea Shoppe, two trim gray-haired ladies ate an early supper at a window table, under a row of hanging red geraniums.

"It's a long trip," Mum said. "I'm glad we didn't try to make it in one day."

"Take the next right," said Annette.

Mum parked in front of three long, identical buildings arranged to form an open courtyard. Each was three stories high.

"Ours is the one that's parallel to the street," said Mum. "Top floor, left, on the back."

"At least there's some trees," said Annette. Three maples were dropping their orange leaves onto the courtyard lawn.

8

The apartment, white and compact, smelled of fresh paint.

"I'll take this room, since sometimes I'll have to sleep during the day," said Mum. It was the smaller, darker bedroom. Annette's had an eastern as well as a northern window. The eastern window looked out, across garbage cans, a strip of concrete, and a board fence, to the back of what looked like another apartment complex. But the northern view had a fir tree. When Annette flopped flat on the bed, all she could see was sky and the treetop.

Mum stood in the doorway, frowning. "I'm sure we can get you a secondhand desk and a bookcase. We'll try to get as fixed up as we can this weekend, shall we? Since we start in at work and school on Monday."

Annette sat up and leaned against the wall. "It's bigger than my room at home. *Much* bigger than my room at Granmaw's."

Mum looked relieved. "Let's unload the car. We can unpack tomorrow."

They made a dozen trips to the car and ate a pizza for supper. Mum gave Annette a bedtime hug. "Don't stay up late," she said. "We'll have a lot to do tomorrow."

Annette was too tired to think about staying up late. She opened her suitcase for her pajamas. There on top, wrapped inside a pair of corduroys, was her father's photograph. She put it on the dresser before she went to sleep.

| ♦ |

Two eggs sunny-side. Bacon, muffins, marmalade. Even a couple of fried tomato slices and a whole pot of tea. "What's all this?" Annette asked.

9

Mum was bustling more than usual. "Something special for your first day. Aren't you hungry? Too nervous to eat?"

Annette almost said, But you haven't fixed breakfast for me since sixth grade. And you know I like porridge, coffee, and toast with cheese. Then she realized how excited Mum was.

"I can always eat," Annette said. But when she sat down in front of the eggs, they glared up at her. She tried the toasted English muffin with raisins. At least it wasn't staring.

The phone rang. While Mum talked in the living room, Annette cut into both eggs, smeared some yolk on her plate, and then forked them into the plastic bag the muffins had come in. While she was at it, she put in the bacon and tomatoes, too. The whole mess sat warm and greasy in her lap while she nibbled the muffin and drank her tea. Her back was toward Mum, but Mum could still see into the kitchen.

"Who was on the phone?" Annette asked casually when Mum returned.

"A person from work, asking me to bring in some information they need. I think second shift is going to be lovely. I have the whole morning free, though it bothers me that I won't be here when you get home. You can call me on my break—the number's on the fridge. Great Scott, look how late it is! Where's your knapsack? Have you got your key?" In the flurry, Annette slipped the eggs into her blazer pocket while Mum was practically pushing her out the door. "You're going to miss that bus. Hurry up! Run!"

Hurry up. It was not a Nootka idea, not a Nootka expression, not Nootka in any way at all.

But Annette ran, her knees pumping up the city street

10

and sweat breaking out under her bangs. Past a boutique, a dry cleaner, a tea shop, a little park of roses. On toward the bus stop at the top of the rise. Her feet felt annoyed in their stiff new shoes. The knapsack of books banged her back as though they wanted her to open up and let them in. Up ahead, at the intersection, she saw the bus arrive. Please, I would like to get on, she prayed to whatever gods might be listening—Granmaw had told her there were always some around. If you are not too busy doing more important things, could you please let me catch that bus?

A short, heavy woman in a dark blue suit approached the bus stop. As she did, she raised her hand, commanding the bus to wait. It obeyed. Deliberately, the woman walked toward the steps. Deliberately, she switched a wicker basket to her left hand. Then she slowly mounted the steps like a person accustomed to having public transport wait for her, like a queen accepting her due. She even wore a crown of yellow braids pinned to the top of her head. Her unhurried boarding gave Annette a few extra seconds. She scrambled, breathless, up the steps.

With a roar, the bus pulled away. Annette fumbled with the fare Mum had thrust into her hand as she had run out the door. She found a seat and collapsed into it gratefully. Gerald Jones, at home, had Catch-a-Bear as his Nootka name. She thought she should be Catch-a-Bus, though only hunters got such names. Still, the idea made her smile.

The bus wound its way along unfamiliar streets. She counted the blocks and watched the street signs as though she were spotting warblers, shy and hard to see. At last she spied the group of massive buildings and the iron fence and gate. The woman with the wicker basket got off first and walked up the sidewalk in a businesslike, teacherish way. Annette supposed she should follow her brisk example, but instead she lingered on the street, peering at the towering walls of gray stone and red brick.

Each window had an arch over it like an eyebrow, so the windows looked like rows of dark, staring eyes. They reminded her of the eye design Granmaw and Mary Jones wove into the edges of their baskets, but the basket eyes were welcoming and the window eyes were not.

Thinking of Granmaw and Mary, Annette did more than remember. For a little while she was at home again, on the front porch of Granmaw's trailer, watching the hands of the two old women, seeing the rushes, smelling the pungent scent of the half-woven baskets. While she was "there," time on the sidewalk stopped.

Then her mind darted away from the pain of missing Granmaw and landed her back in front of the tall iron gate. She should go in. But fear made it hard for her to breathe, let alone walk. She wished some other students would come along. She glanced down the street, tempted to follow the sidewalk as far as it went, anywhere away from St. John's Academy.

Just then a boy came down the sidewalk, wearing a blazer like hers, with the same crest and motto on the pocket: *Per Ardua Ad Astra*. He was tall. He had shiny blond hair that fell over his high, clear forehead like a waterfall. He swung along on confident legs, hungrily smoking a cigarette. At the stone gatepost, he took a final drag, stubbed out the butt, and kicked it furtively into the bushes out of sight. Then he straightened his tie and strode up the school sidewalk, looking as though he owned the place. He looked as though he *were* St. John's Academy.

12

Annette thought he hadn't noticed her till he called back in her direction.

"Everyone gets driven up to the back door," he said. "In vans. Nobody comes in this way."

"Oh," she said.

He smiled. "We're both late on the first day, and all you can say is 'Oh.'" He laughed. "Get marked absent from chapel and you're in big trouble. Better hurry up." He gave her another smile, but he didn't wait for her. He walked quickly up the sidewalk.

There it was again: *hurry up*. But at least the boy's conversation broke the spell that had imprisoned her. Well, she thought, I'm here. I'm not completely invisible—that boy with the waterfall hair saw me. I don't much like being here, but I came a long way and I'm not turning back now.

◊ 3 ◊

Annette crept into the St. John's chapel. It seemed as dim and holy as the pine grove behind the cliff, where in summer the gods sent shafts of light slanting through the fragrant boughs.

But here, a vaulted ceiling replaced the sky, and electric light replaced the sun. Behind the altar, Christ hung suffering on his cross. Row after row of blue blazers packed the room, which smelled of school floor cleanser. Voices raised in excited greetings replaced the rhythmic sounds of the sea.

A teacher with long brown hair motioned with her clipboard. "Class?" she asked. "Name?" She wrote, "Annette Broadhead—W-21" on a gummed tag and stuck it on Annette's lapel. Her breath smelled of peppermint mouthwash. "That's your place for the year," she said. "Hurry now."

Hurry now.

Annette had hardly gotten her knapsack stashed between her feet when everyone stood for the opening hymn. Then they all sat again, with a swoosh of bottoms being lowered into seats—she almost laughed at the sound. The headmaster spoke words of welcome. He prayed, and many voices murmured with him. A choir sang. Annette studied the bearded man in the stained-glass window behind the crucifix. She guessed he was St. John. Why did he hold a dish and a snake? What kind of snake was it?

She wished the activity would stop; she wished for calm and quiet. But everyone had to stand again, and sit down again, and then before there was a chance for her to settle her thoughts, everyone jumped up and rushed away.

Annette consulted her schedule. How strange to have "chapel" directly followed by "gym."

She had to undress in front of everyone, and they all had breasts but her. She stood in line in her underwear to be measured and weighed.

"Well, you're certainly small for your age," said the same long-haired teacher with the clipboard. Her name tag said she was Ms. Pamela Havens, Physical Education Department. "I hope we're going to have a wonderful year together, girls," Ms. Havens told the class in an anxious, squeaky voice. Back at the lockers, Annette saw an angry-looking girl glance her way and mutter to her friend, "Who's that little Injun?" The friend shrugged her heavyset shoulders.

Math class was a blur.

Recess. A flock of blue blazers in front of the snack machines. By the time Annette realized she could go outdoors, a deafening bell clanged for everyone to come in. Nobody seemed bothered by the harsh, horrible noise. Everyone scurried off.

15

In English, Mrs. Greenwood wore her gray hair in snails. Some were coiled on her head. Others marched across her forehead in a straight unsnaillike row. A gold filling in her eyetooth glittered. So did her glasses on a silver chain around her neck, and her pearly button earrings, and the round gold pin at her collar with a profile of Queen Elizabeth inside.

Mrs. Greenwood assigned everyone a partner. She called Annette and her partner "Pair Number One." "Interview each other," she said. "Then you'll introduce each other to the class."

Annette was matched with Katie Danbor, a chunky girl with reddish brown hair, pale skin, and freckles. They eyed each other's name tags.

"You new?" Katie asked. Annette nodded.

"Me, too. I guess it's okay. I'm not sure yet."

"Me, neither," said Annette. "It sure is different."

"Do you know when's lunch? I'm starving. I was in such a hurry this morning I didn't have breakfast."

"I was too nervous to eat," said Annette. "Oh!" she said. "I just remembered something." She put her hand in her blazer pocket. Sure enough, there were the eggs.

Katie said, "My mother makes the best pastry, filled with apricots. We're Ukrainian. What did you remember?"

Annette wondered whether it was safe to tell. "My mum did up a fancy breakfast that I couldn't eat. I didn't want to hurt her feelings so I put it in a plastic bag while she was on the phone. It's still in my pocket."

"Oh, no!" said Katie, grinning. "So what are you going to do with it?"

"I don't know."

"You could just chuck it in the wastebasket when class is over."

"My granmaw wouldn't like that. She says food is sacred. She puts her scraps out for the birds and her peelings in a compost pile. The gods punish waste, she says."

"Gods?"

"Nootka gods. My mother's English. My father was a Nootka."

"Gidú—my grandpa—thinks like your granmaw," Katie said. "He's real old and he helped overthrow the tsar and then the Soviets took over and were just as bad. That's when he left the Ukraine and came here. He keeps a compost pile, too, and he gives his scraps to Roger, his dog. What'cha got in there?"

"Eggs and bacon, mostly."

"Time for the introductions," Mrs. Greenwood said. Annette was startled by her interrupting voice. She and Katie had hardly begun.

"Pass 'em over," Katie whispered.

Annette slipped her the bag. "That red stuff is tomatoes," she whispered.

"Looks yucky, but Roger isn't picky."

"All right, Pair Number One," said Mrs. Greenwood crisply.

Katie took another look at Annette's name tag. "This is Annette Broadhead. She's a new student and is hoping for a wonderful year."

Annette said, "This is Katie Danbor. She's also a new student. She's also hoping for a wonderful year."

"Is that all?" said Mrs. Greenwood. Her eyebrows rose on her forehead, practically touching her first row of snails.

17

Katie flashed Annette a conspiratorial look. "That's all," she said politely. "We didn't have much time."

While a boy in Pair Six was speaking, a bell rang. He stopped in midsentence. The students pushed back their chairs and jumped up. The room emptied in seconds. When Annette rose to leave, even Mrs. Greenwood had disappeared.

"First lunch," her schedule said. The smell of food and a sign in the hallway led her to the basement. A large, noisy room. A line to stand in, a wet tray. Not realizing that she could help herself to the salads and sandwiches, Annette pushed her tray along in a daze. A big woman in white plunked spaghetti onto a plate, ladled on sauce and two meatballs, and handed it over.

Annette found her way to an empty space at the end of a long table. The sauce bled weakly into the puddle of water beneath the lukewarm spaghetti. The inside of one meatball was slightly green. Annette's head began to ache. She drank some milk and ate a piece of bread. The angry-looking girl from gym sat at the other end of the table. She glanced at Annette and whispered to her heavyset friend. The friend looked at Annette and whispered back. Then they both laughed.

Annette's schedule said next she had a double period for art. She went early. The room was large, bright, and empty except for a rumpled man eating a sandwich at his desk. "Come in," he said. "We won't be doing anything for a bit, but make yourself at home. The window seat's nice at this time of day."

Annette put her knapsack on the floor. From the window seat she gazed across the lawn to a dainty tree covered with scarlet stars.

"A Japanese maple," the man said. "I'm Mr. Swanson. You, your label says, are Annette Broadhead."

Annette remembered what Mum had been teaching her about looking into people's eyes when she spoke to them, though to Granmaw such behavior was wrong and rude. "Hello," she said. She motioned toward the tree with her hand. "May I go out?"

The art room had double doors, opening onto the lawn and propped open with a couple of gesso cans. "Of course," Mr. Swanson said.

With her back to the building, she sat beneath the tree, looking up into its starry heavens. After a while, Mr. Swanson stood before her.

"Feel better?"

"Yes," she said, wondering how he knew she had been feeling bad.

Mr. Swanson handed her a pad and a couple of pencils. "This tree might like you to draw it."

Other students drifted out onto the lawn with pads and pencils, but nobody else chose her tree. If bells rang, she didn't hear them. She was surprised when Mr. Swanson said, "You probably have another class to go to. See you tomorrow, Annette."

She could have stayed the rest of the day with the tree, but she collected her things and consulted her schedule once again. The classroom took a bit of finding, but when she reached it she was relieved to see Katie Danbor sitting in the front row and beckoning her to come in and sit down. A few kids were scattered about. No teacher yet.

"You know why we're here, don't you?" Katie whispered.

All Annette knew was that this room number and "Anthro I" were printed on her schedule. "Why?" she said.

"This is the class for dumbbells. If they don't think you can do a foreign language, they stick you in anthro."

"Oh," said Annette. She didn't mind. She had no desire to tackle Latin, German, Spanish, or French. At this school they even had Greek.

Katie turned around in her chair to greet a few other kids. "Hi, Dawn. Hi, Shara. Hi, Jeff." Annette noticed that Dawn was the girl from gym who had made the remark. And her friend was Shara.

"Kids from my old school," Katie whispered, turning back to Annette. "Three winners. Jeff Campbell's not so bad, I guess, but Shara Stone and Dawn Mann are just plain mean. There was a hair-pulling fight in the bathroom last year. A girl saw Shara cheating on a history exam and she told the teacher—he picked three pages of names and dates right out of Shara's lap. Talk about dumb. But Shara tried to get everyone to believe she was innocent. She and Dawn ganged up on the girl who told in the girls' bathroom—it was really awful. I couldn't believe they'd be that nasty."

Annette took another quick glance at the girls Katie was talking about. Shara Stone's shoulders looked weighted down by her heavy breasts. Annette hoped when hers came they wouldn't be such big ones. Dawn's eyes were willful and her mouth pouted. The tall, pimply guy Katie had greeted as Jeff just seemed shy. In a back corner, gazing out the window, Annette spotted the same brown, plump Indian boy she'd seen somewhere earlier in the day. In English, maybe? In the blurry math class? He was staring out the window. To him the classroom, almost full now, didn't seem to exist. He didn't glance her way.

20

"At my old school, Dawn arrived every day in a limousine," Katie whispered. "I mean, la-di-da. But she's not in the Cricket Club. I think she'd trade the limo to get in. It's probably going to be the same here as at my old school. The Cricket Club kids think they own the world."

Annette's head was spinning. A club for people who collected crickets? Before she could ask, the person who had to be their teacher strode into the classroom and closed the door behind her. Annette knew her. She was the woman who had held the bus that morning while Annette raced up the hill.

◇ 4 ◇

She was a short, fat gnome of a woman, with her yellow hair braided into a nest on the top of her head and a hump between her shoulder blades like a witch. The gnome wore a shapeless dark blue suit that looked as though it had been stitched together out of ancient St. John's blazers. A watch hung on a chain around her neck like a referee's whistle. Her eyes pierced at the class through round bifocals with pale pink frames. Her face reminded Annette of a jowly pug dog.

After attendance, the gnome picked up a piece of chalk and printed "Miss Doud" on the board in big, clear letters. Then, the gnome announced her name in a low, scratchy, definite voice.

"I am Genevieve Doud," she said. "Miss Doud to you. Miss, not Ms. This is Anthropology I. Anthropology is the science of man, as in mankind—habits, beliefs, arts, customs, laws. It includes fears, clothing, and what people eat for dinner. During this course, you will each do a project studying your own people, the ones that came before you, your ancestors. I hope you are prepared to work extremely hard, to the best of your ability and even beyond. I also hope you possess the two most important curiosities—intellectual and ethical. Intellectual curiosity means you want to know what is true. Ethical curiosity means you want to know what is good."

Annette, tired now at the end of this strange new day, had thought she would slip into a quiet daydream, but she found herself listening in spite of herself. A project about her Nootka ancestors—that could be fun. Though maybe Mum would want her to research the other side of the family. They had cut Mum off, pretty much, when she married an Indian.

"Let me tell you my view of learning," Miss Doud went on. "Learning is not easy. It requires suffering, even pain. Anyone who tells you different is lying. But I know, and I believe because I have witnessed it time and again, that there is no concept so difficult that it will not eventually give way before the repeated attacks of a mediocre mind. Mediocre minds are what all of us in this room and most people in the world have to work with. Genius is a rare commodity. Genius, in fifteen-year-olds, is almost never recognized. Albert Einstein and Winston Churchill were terrible high-school students. They flunked their courses. They upset their parents. Their teachers considered them failures. They had to wait until they grew up for people to acknowledge their brilliance."

As she listened, Annette stopped seeing a pug dog or a gnome. She began to see Miss Doud, and clearly Miss Doud was a voice and a mind. She had every student in the room listening to her. Annette also had the weird feeling that Miss Doud might have some Nootka blood. That

23

stuff about how learning required pain—that sounded like something Granmaw might have said.

"But genius is not really our concern," Miss Doud continued. "What you and I are concerned with, in this room together, is learning. After the suffering and pain, my young scholars, comes the pleasure of learning, a pleasure of the mind, a pleasure of a lasting kind. Learning is not a materialistic pleasure. It is not based on the possession of things, a goal with which our culture has undoubtedly made you all too familiar.

"You are also familiar with transitory, instant pleasures. Television is one. Drugs and alcohol are another. So are casual, meaningless sexual encounters. Or a bag of chips and an ice-cold Coke—quickly eaten, quickly enjoyed, quickly gone."

A rustle of hunger and understanding ran through the room. Annette realized she was starving. She'd like a slice of the English tea cake Mum had made—there was a big piece left in the apartment fridge. Or one of Katie's mother's fruit-filled pastries, or . . . just about anything.

Miss Doud riveted her eyes on Annette's. Annette knew the teacher had noticed her attention was wandering. It was as though she were aiming her next sentences right at Annette.

"Does school sometimes seem like a jail to you? Do you sometimes feel like a prisoner? A prisoner in a jail has no access to transitory pleasures, but he can sustain himself by reaching into his well-stocked mind. You, also, can sustain yourself in whatever prison you inhabit by stocking the cupboard of your mind with learning, which has ultimate meaning and stands the test of time. That is what I have to offer you, in the last class of your long school day when you are eager for the bell so you can escape. I offer no chips or Cokes, but the pain and pleasure of learning, which will last you a lifetime."

Annette was surprised to hear this teacher talking about school feeling like a jail. It had certainly looked like that to her this morning as she stood on the sidewalk outside the gate. She didn't think teachers liked to admit that students might feel that way.

The sharp bespectacled eyes caught Annette's slightly embarrassed gaze. "What did I just say, Miss Broadhead? Please summarize my remarks."

Annette was startled to be picked out of the group and to have her name already known. But there was something flattering about being called on by Miss Doud.

"You said we'll study our ancestors. You said . . . learning lasts. And it's hard work but fun."

"*Fun,*" said Miss Doud, considering. "*Fun* is a word for a circus or a party, perhaps. Not the right word for this occasion, but you have the gist, Miss Broadhead. You understood the essence. Now, you and your fellow scholars may take out your notebooks and begin to write. I'm about to explain in more detail what anthropology is and how we will approach it in this class. You will have a written quiz on these remarks tomorrow. The quiz will count. For it you must know three things. You must know how to spell *anthropology.* You must be able to define anthropology. You must be able to give an example of what an anthropologist does."

In school last year with Mr. Feeney, at the mention of a quiz, somebody would have been sure to let out a groan. Probably Kiki. He never did any schoolwork, so he hated to have a quiz. Here, in Miss Doud's class, the only response to the announcement was a rustle of notebooks and the click of ball-point pens.

25

Once she had her notebook open, Annette glanced quickly around the room, curious to see how everyone looked, now that they were about to get down to business. Katie was all set. Even Dawn and Shara looked grudgingly ready. Mostly, Annette wanted to see the Indian boy. He was still gazing fixedly out the window. He had no paper and nothing to write with. Don't shame us, Annette thought. Don't make us look bad here in this foreign place, even if it feels like a jail to you. For heaven's sake, at least try. But the boy kept looking out the window, and Annette had to turn around and focus all of her attention on taking notes. Miss Doud was already beginning her lecture, and she wasn't going slowly, either.

◊ 5 ◊

Annette hesitated outside the door of the computer room. It was in the library basement, bright with fluorescent lights, lined with screens and keyboards. Wall-to-wall carpet, no windows, no air. Not her kind of place. But she had an assignment.

Only one other kid was there, in this hour right after school. Most people had sports or clubs. It looked like Katie Danbor's back. Since school had started two weeks ago, she'd been friendly in the classes they shared. On the second day of English she'd told Annette, "Roger loved the eggs." But Annette had never seen her anywhere else. Maybe Katie was just nice to everyone.

Annette chose a computer next to Katie's and hung her blazer on the back of its chair.

"Hi!" Katie looked up from the screen. "Don't you hate these bloody uniforms?" Katie's blazer lay on the floor in a heap.

Annette was grateful for clothes that made her look like

everyone else. Back home, she wore mostly thin-kneed corduroys and faded sweatshirts from the Salvation Army store.

"I don't mind them," she said.

"Well, most people hate them," Katie said. "I heard a group of students tried to get rid of them last year, but no luck." Frowning at her screen, Katie went back to her clack-clacking.

Mary Jones, Granmaw's friend up home, had made a special point of reminding Annette, before she left for Victoria, "You can't trust whites. Ever." Annette knew Mary Jones wasn't right. After all, Mum was white. But it was confusing to have Mary's advice come into her mind sometimes, even when she didn't want it there. Maybe Katie couldn't really like a person who . . . liked uniforms.

"Bet you're here to do Greenwood's 'letter to a friend,'" Katie said. Mrs. Greenwood had told the class they could learn word processing "in five minutes." She'd said it was a "required part of this course in communication."

Green print covered Katie's screen. Annette had never used a computer.

"Is that your letter?" Annette asked.

"Just about finished." Katie pressed a couple of keys and a nearby machine started to type all by itself, startling Annette.

"Neat, huh?" Katie said. "My dad's a newspaper editor. He has a laser printer at home and a computer with a hard disk. But he doesn't let anybody into his office, not even my mother. Did your school have this same kind of stuff?"

"No computers at all. We only had twelve kids in eighth and ninth grades combined."

"Gee. Really small." Katie's letter finished printing. She tore it out of the machine. "I wrote to my friend back in my old school. It's funny being here without her. We talk on the phone, but it's not the same when you're not doing the same things. The kids who transferred here with me—well, I told you, they're not my favorite people."

"I thought I'd write to my friend up home. Florence."

"I could help you get started. Then I have to get out of here. It's my day to stop at Gidú's house on the way home. He'll be expecting me. We sit under his plum tree and listen to the leaves fall. In spring, we watch the buds open."

"Tell Roger hello."

"You should have seen him scarf down those eggs. He practically ate the bag."

Katie quickly showed Annette how to follow the steps written on big posters around the room. "Bye," she said, scooping her knapsack and blazer from the floor where she'd dumped them. "See you tomorrow, Annette. You and me versus Greenwood and Doud." Katie grinned.

Slowly Annette smiled back. "Bye!" she called.

It took half an hour to write and print her letter, but Annette was able to figure everything out. She wrote:

Dear Florence,

Well, here I am at St. John's Academy. It's okay. How are you? Fine, I hope. I'll see you at Christmas vacation. If it ever comes. Tell Granmaw hello. Please write to me.

Your friend,
Annette

29

She made two copies, one for Mrs. Greenwood and one for Florence. The letter looked nice, but Annette knew it didn't say anything important. It certainly didn't "communicate."

Late some nights when Mum was asleep, the throbbing hum of the city and a vague, unsettling tension kept Annette awake. Then she sent her need for Granmaw out her north window, past the fir tree, back to the trailer on the other side of the island—and received an answer in reply. Even at that distance, hours away, Granmaw's spirit could make Annette feel calm, like an unruffled pond. She couldn't send Granmaw a letter. Granmaw couldn't read.

But she knew Mrs. Greenwood, who wore the same metallic jewelry every day and the same gray snails lined up in rows, didn't have that kind of communicating in mind. She wanted a written letter and she took a point off for each misspelled word.

Riding home on the bus, Annette imagined another letter to Florence, one that was so real she knew she'd never write or send it:

> It's okay here, but I miss you and Granmaw and home. Sometimes so much I have to tighten my muscles hard to keep from crying. There's only one other Indian kid from over west, Joe Martin, but he hardly talks to anyone, let alone me, even though we have classes together. I don't like him because he acts dumb, and I don't want people to think our people are dumb. At the Freshman Mixer the chaperons made me ask Joe to dance. It was awful—his legs are so wide he can hardly move them. We don't have anything in common

except being Indian. It was like trying to dance with a stuffed bear.

Art class is quiet and good. In another class I'm going to study my family and its history.

Getting undressed for gym is the worst. Here they don't just play outside at recess. They have gym. Everyone has tits but me. In the locker room some kids have started calling me "the little Injun." Dawn Mann started it. She giggles and pretends it isn't an insult, but it is.

One girl is very nice. Katie.

At home, Mum is busy with her job. Some things are the same for Mum and me here, like wearing uniforms all day and learning to use computers. Mum also goes to classes to learn how to start IV's and give new drugs. She has a new friend, Dr. Peter Harris. After she's had lunch with him, she hums around the apartment and peeks in the mirror, patting her hair. When he doesn't call, she mopes. Then she squares her shoulders and reminds me how to act and to make good grades. "Study hard and don't lose your scholarship," she says. I don't tell her the bad stuff. I don't want to worry her, I want to make it on my own. But sometimes I don't care if I make it—I just want to come home. I miss you and Granmaw and Kiki, the water and the hemlock trees. The wind. The fog. Air. I can't watch the fog because there's always other things I should do, like hurry to school or pay attention to the math problems on the board. The air here doesn't smell right, and everything is too fast.

31

They even play music in the elevators. Please write to me.

Your best friend,
Annette

◇ 6 ◇

Mum's note on the kitchen table said, "Night shift again—horrors. Leftover casserole, and you can make a salad. Ice cream in freezer. On a whim, I made some fudge sauce—jar, second shelf, fridge."

Fudge sauce! Annette didn't like coming home to an empty house, but it was nice of Mum to try to make it up to her.

Next to the note lay a letter, from Florence. It wasn't thick. But it was an honest-to-goodness letter. Annette ripped it open and zoomed right past the "Dear Annette." It said:

> Thanks for writing. We're mostly fine, only not really, because I heard that boy Mike who started in school with us is dead of bad drugs down in Seattle. And that other boy from our last year's class, Jakey, hitched down to L.A. and disappeared. Nobody's heard from him. Nobody

knows what happened to him. Ma says she's not going to let that happen to Tom. She says boys have a harder time than girls, but I'm not so sure. She's been canning pumpkin, so the windows are all steamed up. She's got another kid to baby-sit now, and she's having another baby herself. There's just no room—I swear I'm moving out. I do bottles but not diapers. I can't stand baby poop. Tom took the potatoes out of their bag and spread them around. On the windowsills, the couch. Even one on the rocking chair. Wilma's starting to crawl. Gino's been okay though no fish. I go to Granmaw's every day for news. Sometimes we talk about you— your ears should be burning. She says to tell you she's here.

That's all, except that I guess Kiki's my boyfriend now. I mean, he really is. So everything's different. But I'm

Still your friend,
Florence

Kiki? Florence's boyfriend? Annette couldn't take it in.

She couldn't recall that boy, Mike, very well. But Jakey she remembered, though he'd stopped coming to school after the first week. He'd been older and bigger than the rest of them and he hadn't fitted in. She'd been a little scared of him. Now he had disappeared.

She opened the fridge and looked at the fudge sauce, but all at once she wasn't really hungry. In the living room she sat down as if to read the funnies, the way she always did when she came home from school. But instead, she read Florence's letter again, and its pictures began to form in her mind.

She saw Florence's mother wearing one of Gino's plaid flannel shirts that wouldn't button over her big pregnant belly. Her seashell ashtray overflowed. She was canning pumpkin, rinsing the seeds in a dented, two-legged colander. Annette had never seen that colander when it had all three of its legs. Vera roasted the seeds with oil and salt, and her family ate them like peanuts.

Annette also saw the babies, Tom intent on the potatoes, Wilma crawling on her fat little arms and legs. The two who came to be baby-sat and now a new one as well. Vera and Florence fed the little ones bottles on the couch. The bigger ones sat in front of the old black-and-white TV working on their thumbs. Watching cartoons. The picture was terrible, faint and snowy. She and Florence used to watch cartoons on it, too, and when they complained about the picture, Vera told them they were lucky to have a TV at all.

No fish, but Gino was okay. That meant he was asleep in the bedroom, or fixing up his boat, or tinkering in his workshop, not out on a binge. Gino didn't drink often. But every few months, he disappeared for a few days.

Going to Granmaw's for news meant the shortwave radio from the fishing boats, plus the Vancouver weather report. Granmaw's children, except for her one son, Artie, had grown up and gone off island. But Artie had given Granmaw a good radio. He brought her fish, game birds, and venison. He fixed her wooden steps when they rotted. Neighbors brought her cans of coffee and condensed milk when they came by for news from the radio, and then stayed to drink a cup. Granmaw raised vegetables, which she dried and canned. She picked wild blueberries, raspberries, and grapes. People came to her for cures and medicines. Sometimes they sent for her to deliver babies. They paid in sugar, oil, and flour. She got by.

Granmaw's face would be good for the new art project. At school now, Mr. Swanson had the class working from photographs, making drawings and then woodcuts. Annette wished she had a photograph of Granmaw, but Granmaw would never let her picture be taken, not even a snapshot or a Polaroid. Annette knew she would never forget how Granmaw looked. She was very old, flat faced, big knuckled, and gap toothed. Dents and gullies crisscrossed her leathery brown skin. Thick nails, strong as eagle claws, tipped her knotty hands. She kept her white-streaked hair behind her big ears and tied it at the nape of her neck. She didn't have a whole lot of neck. When Annette had noticed that her deep brown irises were rimmed with blue and that the whites were turning yellow, she'd asked Granmaw why. "Rainbow eyes," Granmaw had said. "You wait long enough, you'll have them, too. Rainbows around your green eyes. Green eyes that are the eyes of an old soul."

At last, after circling round and round it, Annette took in the real news of the letter and felt a pang of jealousy. Kiki had been her friend, too, or almost more a brother than a friend. She'd always known him and Florence. They'd grown up together, digging in the sand, throwing rocks, making forts in the woods. Tag, hide-and-seek. Doctor, kissing games. Last year, they'd been a three-some, clamming, rowing out in Gino's dinghy to fish, shooting at tin cans in the woods. Once they'd gotten a bottle of cheap pink wine and drunk it fast, then all gotten sick, puking in the weeds together. Annette had said she'd never drink any wine again, and Kiki had laughed at her and called her a baby.

She tried to imagine Florence and Kiki kissing. Or more. "I mean, he really is. So everything's different."

She'd been lost in her thoughts so long the sun had gone down and she hadn't noticed. She turned on some lights in the dark apartment. Mum's note was still on the kitchen table. Fudge sauce "on a whim." Like *hurry up*, it was not a Nootka idea. But now a whim hit Annette, and she reached for the St. John's directory and dialed Katie's number.

"Hey, is that really you?" Katie said into her ear. "Neat-o."

"It's really me," Annette said. "I just heard from my friend Florence up home. Did I ever tell you about Florence and Kiki and me?"

"Just a sec," Katie said. Annette heard Katie make a muffled request to someone to hang up in a minute. Then she heard Katie pick up an extension, and the click of the downstairs phone. "I'm in my room now," Katie said. "On my bed, actually. The cord on the hall phone is three miles long. But I don't have a whole bunch of time before I have to help get dinner. Who are Florence and Kiki?"

"Florence was my best friend up home. Florence and Kiki and I hung around together. Now Kiki is Florence's boyfriend."

"Oh, poop. How can they do that to you?"

"I don't know. Can you hang on a second?" Annette got an emery board from her room and sat down with it on the carpet. She wedged a sofa cushion between her and the wall. Mum had been showing her how to file her nails. "I'm back," she said.

37

"So," said Katie. "Tell. What is Florence like and what is Kiki like and how come they're together?"

"It's weird to talk about."

"That's okay. I'll ask zillions of questions. All you have to do is answer."

Behind Katie's voice, Annette heard a knock and then another voice. "Now?" said Katie with a hand over the phone. "Already?" Then, to Annette, "I have to help with dinner now, wouldn't you know. Rats."

"That's okay."

"Tell me tomorrow."

"Okay. See you. Bye."

The casserole Mum had mentioned turned out to be Annette's favorite, shell pasta with cheese, ham, mushrooms, and peas. She made a salad and sat down with the funnies to eat. Fudge sauce to look forward to. Yum.

◇ 7 ◇

Annette woke with Miss Doud's words ringing in her ears. The assignment was the first part of the ancestor project.

"Bring an object to class, something important to the culture of your ancestors, and explain its meaning as an anthropologist would explain it," Miss Doud had said. "On the board, I want you to list where you got your information. That means written sources, video sources, and people."

Today, Annette's report was due. She couldn't eat breakfast. During first lunch, Dawn and Shara stood in front of her in the line.

"We're going to L.A. for the holidays," Dawn announced in a loud, showy voice. "My father's taking the whole family to Disneyland."

Shara's voice rang out. "We're going to Hawaii. As usual. To our beach house. My mother won't hear of going anywhere else." They both looked at Annette. Dawn leaned over to whisper in Shara's ear and Annette overheard, as she was intended to, something about not wanting to get too much sun because Dawn didn't want to look "black as an Indian."

Annette looked at her own brown arm. Was that brown—that pretty brown, *her* brown—what Dawn meant by black, which she said with such distaste? Annette left the line and went early to art class, where Mr. Swanson always had crackers and tea if anyone wanted them. Though today she couldn't even eat crackers and tea. Art class, which she usually loved, went by in a haze of apprehension. She walked through the halls to anthropology with a sense of dread.

At least she wasn't first. Nearly all of the class had reported—sly Miss Doud had had them start at the end of the alphabet and work up to the beginning. Now Jeff Campbell, tall as a hat rack and nearly as thin, stood by Miss Doud's wicker basket. He held up a pair of argyle socks. People snickered and Jeff looked embarrassed. Annette prayed that nobody would snicker when her turn came.

"My grandmother knit these," he said. "Her mother, who was born near Glasgow, Scotland, taught her how when she was six years old. My sister, who's twenty-two, can't knit at all and my grandmother thinks that's terrible. She said to me when I was interviewing her"—Jeff read the next words from a three-by-five card—"'Your sister should be ashamed of herself, with a fine name like Fiona Campbell, and never to knit an argyle in her life!'"

A few people laughed and Jeff looked relieved. Annette felt a certain sympathy for Fiona. Granmaw had tried to teach her some of the old Indian ways. It was fun learning some of them, but she'd also learned how to make herself scarce and avoid Granmaw's lessons.

40

"My great-great-grandmother's family raised sheep near Glasgow," Jeff continued. "They sheared them and spun yarn from the wool. Some wool was sold and some was used at home. All the girls learned to knit when they were really young. It was a skill girls were supposed to have if they wanted to get some guy to marry them or something. I guess it meant the guy wouldn't have to go without socks."

Some of the boys cheered. Katie groaned. "People will do anything to keep women down," she whispered to Annette. Jeff smiled, and his embarrassment faded. He looked as though he was starting to enjoy himself a little.

"My clan, which is sort of like a tribe, is the Campbells of Argyll County. That's in the central western section of Scotland, north and west of Glasgow." Jeff paused and drew a rough map on the board. Annette was surprised he could do it so well—he must have practiced. It was amazing how hard people were working in this class. Nobody wanted to get up in front of the whole group—and especially Miss Doud—and look like a fool.

"So, where was I?" Jeff consulted his little pile of cards. "Oh, yes—the colors and diamond pattern of these socks comes from the Campbell clan plaid, or tartan. It's wool cloth specially dyed and woven to represent the Campbells. It wasn't for everyday—just for weddings and funerals and wars and stuff. Today lots of people buy argyle-style socks at Eaton's and MacLeod's, and people who aren't even Scotspeople wear them. But they're not the real thing, the way these are. To an anthropologist, *these* socks mean a lot. They show what my ancestors raised on their farm, how they made a living, what they expected girls to do, and what they wore for part of their—their ceremonial dress. My source was Mrs. Angus Campbell. And I got the

41

map from our Rand McNally atlas at home." He wrote his sources on the board.

"Well done, Mr. Campbell," said Miss Doud. All the other teachers called their students by their first names. Katie didn't like Miss Doud's formality, but Annette did. "Mr. Campbell" made Jeff sound like somebody.

Even before Miss Doud gave her judgment, Annette was impressed by Jeff's report. He'd found so much to say about just a pair of socks! In fact, Annette had been impressed by everyone in the class and was not sure she could do as well. Muffy Anderson had given everyone pieces of homemade salt-rising bread, with home-churned butter, which was her friend Lisa Smythe's project. They were Cricket Club kids. Annette had learned that cricket was a game like baseball only duller and slower. Some kids' families belonged to a social club in Victoria where it was played. And she had also decided, despite what Katie said about Cricket Club kids in general, that Lisa and Muffy seemed okay.

Katie had done the best report in the class. She'd read about the Ukraine and the Russian Orthodox church so she could explain the meaning of the cross with the knobs on it she wore around her neck. "This cross, which my grandfather gave me on my last birthday, was his engagement gift to my grandmother," she'd said in a quiet but impassioned voice. "My grandfather helped overthrow one dictator, the tsar, and then got stepped on by the Soviets, who were another. He and my grandmother left their parents and their homeland and came to Canada. They were both nineteen. That's just four years older than me—than us." Miss Doud didn't allow applause, but the class had applauded Katie's report anyway.

"And now our final report, from Miss Broadhead," said

Miss Doud. Annette's heart leaped up into her throat like a big, uncomfortable frog.

Annette made her way to the front of the room, wishing she could turn into a frog completely and leap out the window into the autumn rain. She was used to reading a textbook chapter and writing answers to the questions at the end. Or doing twenty math problems that were all pretty much the same. She didn't know how to look things up in books or organize what she found so it made sense. Mum wasn't really a source—she wasn't even a Nootka—and Granmaw was far away.

Joe Martin had also spoiled her report by choosing the same object. He'd brought in two cans of salmon, set them on the floor, and stood on them to show that his whole tribe based its life on the salmon. Miss Doud had chided him for not doing real research and given him a low grade, but he'd gotten a big laugh.

Annette didn't have a clever stunt. She had a picture of a salmon she'd cut from a sports magazine and a few things she'd heard people in the village say about salmon. When she took her place next to Miss Doud's wicker basket, even those shreds of information retreated into a silent cave in her brain and refused to come out.

Eyes stared at her: Katie, Jeff, even Joe, who usually looked out the window all period. Annette wanted to do well—to please them and to *show* them. She clutched her picture of a salmon, but she couldn't think of anything to say. The words would not be coaxed out of the dark cave. She was embarrassed to be smaller and look younger than most of the others, and to be a different color from anyone but Joe. She felt herself start to get angry. Why should I talk to these people about the Nootka anyway? Why

43

should I talk to Dawn Mann, smirking at "the little In-jun"?

"Your ancestors are the same tribe as Joe's, and the salmon has been important to them?" Miss Doud prompted.

Annette nodded.

"Can you tell us anything more? Does your father go out fishing?"

Annette shook her head no.

"Is drying or smoking or preserving salmon an activity your mother does, or your grandmother?"

Annette stood there, silent. She had no way to explain. Mum hated all fish except tuna salad. Annette had never met Mum's mother—because mum had married an In-dian. Granmaw wasn't her father's mother, who was dead, but her godmother. Granmaw sometimes did smoke fish, and Annette had helped, but she didn't want to tell about it. It would sound dumb to these kids who went to Hawaii and bought smoked fish at the deli neatly wrapped. What business of Miss Doud's was it, or of the class's, all these white kids with their light hair and eyes? If only she could recall the words she had planned to say. She had had them memorized on the bus this morning. But unlike Jeff, she didn't have any three-by-five cards, and now the words were still in hiding.

"The life of my people is based upon the salmon," she finally blurted, saying the exact same words Joe had said, and then stared at the floor. Someone tittered and was shushed. The room went very quiet for what seemed a long time. Then Annette heard feet shuffle and bodies shift. Somebody coughed, somebody giggled, somebody muttered.

"Come and see me here during recess tomorrow morn-ing, Miss Broadhead," Miss Doud said. "Class dismissed."

◇ 8 ◇

The note said, "Night shift. Hot dogs? Love, Mum."
Thank goodness Mum wasn't home.

Mum could talk to anyone about anything. She'd gotten
the super to come and fix the faucet. She'd made a speech
at her hospital on "Health Care for Our Native Amer-
icans" and come home triumphant. She chatted on the
phone with her new doctor friend, Peter Harris, all the
while stirring a pudding on the stove. Peter Harris had a
British accent and had been to dinner once. He ate with
his fork wrong side up in his left hand, pushing bites of
meat onto.it with his knife. "Now, you must be in about
the eighth grade," he'd said to Annette, and then apolo-
gized like anything for being off by two years.

Annette hadn't told Mum she had to make the report.
She wasn't going to tell her that she'd failed. She could
hear Miss Doud's low, scratchy voice telling her to come
during recess tomorrow.

What she wanted to hear was wind in pine trees. She

45

wanted to be with Granmaw, who didn't talk much at all. She wanted to see Florence. They could spend a day together at the beach or in the woods and never say a word.

Annette drifted so far away from Victoria that when the phone rang, she scarcely heard it.

"Hi! It rang so long I was afraid you weren't there," said Katie.

"No, I'm here."

"Listen, it won't be so bad tomorrow. I had to go to the principal's office in seventh grade when I said something smart to a teacher, and it turned out okay."

"What did you say?"

"We had this awful sub in history who was running down the Quebecois. I called him a bigot. The principal basically told me I was right but that I couldn't be rude about it—had to respect authority and all that. She was really neat. The sub had told me I couldn't come back to class, which I didn't want to anyway, so the principal and I ate these lemon drops she had in a jar on her desk and talked about Quebec."

"I'm afraid Miss Doud will kill me."

"She's not the killing kind. She's a pusher, not a killer."

"I'm on scholarship. I have to do well."

"Even so. Doud's no dragon. And nobody else will be there. Say, did you notice how I looked straight at Muffy in my report? When I said the Communist party had pretty much swallowed up the Ukraine and my family's religion and that's why my grandfather came here?"

What Annette had noticed about Muffy was that her fine auburn hair curled like a cloud around her face. It made her face look like it was floating. "No," she said.

"Well, she gave me a hard time about my cross. 'What's that funny-looking thing around your neck?' she says to

46

me. So I told her I go to the Ukrainian Orthodox church and that it's a Russian cross. Then she wants to know if I'm a Communist. So I told her I was a mole plotting to overthrow St. John's Academy, the government, and the universe in general. She laughed that ha ha laugh that means she didn't get the joke. She's so dumb. And she wears makeup."

"She does?" Annette said.

"You bet your booties. Just enough to look good and not enough to get into trouble with Ms. Havens." The high-pitched gym teacher wasn't just high-pitched about sports, Annette had found out. She was high-pitched about enforcing every part of the dress code.

"Katie? Meet me by my locker at the start of recess?"

"Sure. I'll be there anyway, but I'll look for you. What for?"

"You know. Just to wish me luck."

| ◆ |

Even with Katie's good-luck wish, Annette felt scared when she approached Miss Doud's room at recess the next day.

"Let me know how it goes," Katie called after her.

"Well, Miss Broadhead." Miss Doud looked up from the papers she was correcting. "How are you today?"

"Fine, thank you, Miss Doud. And how are you?" The words slipped out automatically. Mum was unrelenting about looking people in the eye and "using manners," though that wasn't how you talked to people at home. Annette noticed that Miss Doud seemed a bit surprised—but also pleased.

"I'm very well. Thank you for inquiring. Now, please sit

47

down, make yourself comfortable, and tell me the rest of your report."

Annette wondered how Miss Doud could be so sure that there was more to tell. But of course there was.

"My friend's father, her stepfather, he fishes for salmon. And our other friend, Kiki, he goes out on the boat with him, with Gino. Gino won't take Florence and me. He says women aren't allowed because they scare the fish."

"Go on," said Miss Doud neutrally.

"Kiki says Gino talks a lot on the boat, though he sure doesn't at home. Gino told Kiki it's important not to take too many fish—not to be greedy. Taking too many is the worst thing—very bad. And Gino even talks to the fish."

Miss Doud looked interested. "What does he say?"

"He sort of calls to them, to get them to come to his boat so he can catch them. And after they're caught"— Annette stared at her shoes, hoping Miss Doud wouldn't think that Gino was crazy—"he thanks them."

"Do you know why he does that?"

"He told Kiki his father talked to the fish and thanked the salmon. Talked to them like they were friends and he was sorry they were going to die but he had to feed his family. He says that's what you're supposed to do."

Miss Doud smiled. "Excellent material, Miss Broadhead. Is there anything else?"

Annette nodded. It was all coming easily now. "Sometimes Granmaw smokes the salmon her son Artie brings, if he brings too much. She taught me how to help. My job was to make sure the fire didn't go out or get too hot. She's my godmother, and she also makes baskets. She says they're supposed to be woven so close they hold water. Because in olden times the women heated stones

48

in the fire and put the red-hot stones in the baskets of water and boiled the fish."

"So your godmother—Granmaw—tried to make her own baskets watertight. That's also excellent. The anthropologist Franz Boas would corroborate your findings, Miss Broadhead. You're keeping fine company. Can you analyze your observations as an anthropologist would?"

Analyze. Annette almost said, No, I can't. Then she heard Mum's voice. Mum could back off from anything and sound like a newscaster talking. Annette tried Mum's newscaster voice.

"An anthropologist would see respect for nature in Gino. That my people think you shouldn't be greedy. And that the salmon was important to the Nootka, to catch and eat and survive, long ago and now, today."

"What about Granmaw?"

"The way cooking was done before my people had metal pots." Annette remembered what Jeff had said about girls having to knit socks in his family. "What men did—fish. And what women did—weave baskets to cook the fish. Maybe that could be why Gino won't let Florence and me go on the boat. Because that's just not how it's supposed to be. Men have their job and women have their job and they're both important but they shouldn't get mixed up."

"Yes."

That was all Miss Doud said, but the way she said it made Annette feel like the proud tree on the cliff that held the eagles' nest.

"Next time you report to the class, Miss Broadhead, I want you to look straight at me the way you did today. Eye to eye—until you get into your subject. Then you can look at anyone you like. There are still ten minutes before recess ends. Thank you for your excellent report. You are dismissed."

Miss Doud straightened a stack of papers and uncapped her famous pen that used real green ink. When she handed back papers, all the comments were in green. She was going back to work.

With the word *dismissed* still in her ears, Annette left Miss Doud's classroom. She had heard *You are dismissed* enough that she'd figured it out. Dismissed didn't really mean you *were* anything. It meant something was finished, like a class or a report. She wanted some crackers with peanut butter and a carton of milk. She wanted to find Katie and tell her that Miss Doud had liked the report. She wanted to thank Katie somehow for saying it wouldn't be so bad and making it easier.

But she paused as she approached the stairs to the wide basement hallway outside the cafeteria, where kids munched snacks, talked, and relaxed, their voices and laughter bouncing noisily off the stone walls. Beneath the cheerful din, she seemed to hear Gino's voice murmuring to the fish. She could see Granmaw's leathery hands at work weaving a basket, the swollen knuckles, the broken nails, the sinewy forearms pulling on the rushes. She could see Gino's dark, silent face as he slept, exhausted after days on the boat, on the couch in front of the snowy TV.

Instead of going down to the basement, Annette ducked out the door at the end of the corridor and sat on the stone bench out of sight. Wasps had built a nest under the eaves overhead and nobody had discovered it or bothered to knock it down. In this sheltered nook, the autumn sun was still warm enough to bring the wasps to life. She watched the wasps crawl out, take flight, return to the gray, papery nest, and crawl inside again.

A bell clanged in the corridor, but Annette didn't hear it. She was watching the wasps. She forgot about Mrs. Greenwood's class, which she had next. She didn't hear the warning bell. She didn't hear the late bell. Time slowed and stopped, a time that was never "dismissed." Time was a river, not a log to be sawed into lengths.

Over the low hum of the insects, she heard voices murmuring within her. Vera's voice said, "Don't forget us." Florence's said, "Kiki's my boyfriend now." Mum's voice, loving and prodding, said, "Study hard and keep your scholarship. That school is your way into the world." Gino said nothing—he was too tired and still asleep—but she felt she had betrayed him by telling his secrets. Miss Doud's voice said, "Thank you for your excellent report," while Mary Jones warned, "Keep your business to yourself. All we ever got from whites was sickness, cheating, war, and trouble." Granmaw's message was wordless but it meant that she was always there.

Annette searched for her own voice among them. The others were important. They were part of her. But she didn't want them to drown her out. At last her own voice came, quieter than the rest but clear and just as strong.

Find your own way, it said. You must find your own way.

| ♦ |

Miss Doud's classroom emptied like a bucket turned upside down. "Where were you?" Katie demanded the minute everyone was gone. "I looked for you at the end of recess, but I couldn't find you. And then you didn't show up for English at all!"

51

Annette shook her head to show she couldn't answer right away.

"Did Doud like your report?"

Annette nodded.

"Well, is that *all*? Why weren't you in English? Greenwood made a comment. You'll get a pink slip tomorrow."

Annette had heard about pink slips. One in a week sent you to detention for an hour. Two sent you to your adviser for a lecture and gave you detention for a week. Three meant the headmaster's office, a phone call home, and other serious punishments, usually including probation. She would not tell Mum about the pink slip. She would just serve her time.

"I'll show you," Annette said. They collected their gear. Annette led the way to the door she had found that opened upon her secret retreat. But the day had turned cloudy. The nook between the buildings, so appealing in the sun, seemed chilly and uninviting. The nest hung in its place, but the wasps were nowhere to be seen.

Katie looked around. "This is where you spent fourth period? I thought maybe you nipped down the street to the Malt Shop." Annette had heard of it, a favorite after-school ice-cream parlor.

"No, I was here."

"For a whole period?"

"It didn't seem long. It didn't seem like any time at all. I sort of wasn't really *here*."

"I don't get it," said Katie. Annette knew Katie wanted to understand. It was hard to find language for something wordless. In silence, Annette searched for a way to explain, but Katie found words faster.

"I know—I bet it's like 'walkabout.' Like when aborigines in Australia disappear into the bush for weeks or months at a time. Leave their jobs or whatever. Just kind of check out and come back—whenever. Only you don't actually *go* anywhere except in your head. Maybe it's like that."

Annette nodded.

"Weird," Katie said, not unkindly.

"Nootka," Annette said.

"Do you think you could eat at my house tomorrow?" said Katie suddenly. "It's Friday. No school the next day."

"Probably. My mum'll be at work. I could call tonight and let you know."

"Can I ask you something?"

"Sure."

"Did you have a phone where you lived before?"

"Mum had one at the clinic, with an answering machine. But we didn't have one in the apartment upstairs. Or at Granmaw's, where I stayed a lot."

"I," said Katie, "would die without a phone."

Annette laughed. "No, you wouldn't. Did you ever live without one?"

"Come to think of it, at camp. There was only one phone, in the office, for emergencies."

"Did you die?"

"I guess not."

"Phones are nice," Annette said. "But they're not Nootka."

"That's me," said Katie. She wriggled her shoulders and jumped up and down a couple of times. "Listen," she said. "We've got to do something here. We can't stand around looking at a wasps' nest. Let's go run around the track. You want to?"

"Okay."

"Gym shoes?" said Katie.

"Right."

They collected their gym shoes from the smelly locker room. The track was deserted. They dropped their knapsacks on the ground and started crunching around on the cinders.

"What sports do you do?" Katie asked.

"Nothing. We played softball or volleyball at school, just fooling around. Florence and I used to run places together for fun."

Katie began to puff a little. "The one who's with Kiki now?"

Annette nodded. She'd gotten used to the idea, almost.

"My mother keeps saying, 'There'll be plenty of time for boys,'" said Katie. "But I wish that time would hurry up."

"Me, too."

"I notice Muffy's always surrounded. And Dawn—I saw her chatting up Jeff Campbell in the hall the other day. He kept sort of backing away. It was pretty funny. Is it a mile now? I'm getting a cramp in my calf."

"We've only gone around twice."

"Oh. Well, it's not a bad cramp. I can probably run through it. Let's sprint to the finish once we get to the eighth-of-a-mile line."

Annette hadn't noticed any line. She waited till Katie burst into a fast run and then joined her. For most of the distance to the finish line, Katie was ahead. Then she flagged and Annette easily moved in front of her. At the finish line, Annette had a five-yard lead.

"We could walk one now," Annette said when Katie caught up.

"You're fast," Katie panted.

"I love to run."

"I'll stick to swimming and cricket. At least, that's what

I want to try out for. We didn't have a pool at my old school, but I swim at camp. And I played cricket on our team last year. Of course, there's a lot more competition here."

"It's not Nootka to compete."

"A no-no, huh? Not Nootka. N.N."

Annette smiled. They collected their knapsacks and started across the lawn toward the gate. Annette glanced up at the motto. She'd learned it meant something like "through work to the stars." Waiting with Annette at her bus stop, Katie thumped her fist against her thigh. "We've got to do something here," she said. "We can't let the Dawns and Muffies run the world. There's no fall sport I can go out for, but I think you should go out for field hockey and then in the spring, lacrosse."

The bus appeared around the corner and pulled over for Annette. "I don't know how to play them," she said as she mounted the bus steps.

Katie started walking backward up the street toward her home. "That's okay!" she shouted. "You can learn!"

◈ 9 ◈

Mum was thrilled that Katie had invited Annette to dinner. "Of course you can go!" she said. "And I think you should take something. What's Katie's number? I'll call her mother and see what you can bring. Dessert, maybe? Ice cream, and I could make a chocolate layer cake. . . ."

"Mum," said Annette. "It's just supper, not a potlatch. Besides, I'm going over straight from school, so I can't carry anything."

"Well, that's true. I'm just used to how we did things in the village."

Annette noticed that Mum never called Port West "home," even though she'd lived there many years. Still, in the spirit of matching a host's gifts, Mum put some homemade blueberry jam in Annette's pack. Katie's mother seemed happy to receive it, though it was Katie's little brother, Greg, who eyed the jar and licked his lips. He was chunky like Katie, with even more freckles.

"Will it taste like blueberry pie?"

"Without the crust," Annette said.

"How come your name isn't White Feather?"

"Greg," Katie said.

"Because my mother's mother was named Anne so my mother called me Annette."

"But Katie says you're an Indian."

"I'm half Indian. People who are all Indian have names like everybody else nowadays, though sometimes a man will get a secret tribal name if he does something special like catching a bear."

"Does your father have a tribal name?"

"No."

"Why not?"

"Greg, get lost," said Katie.

"Get lost yourself," said Greg. "Bet you don't know *her* real name. It's Oksanna. Ox. She belongs to the tribe of the Ox."

"Gregor Michael Danbor, I'm gonna kill you."

"Why don't you girls go up to Katie's room?" said Mrs. Danbor. She had short gray hair and a warm smile. Katie had told Annette her mother was a counselor at a college, but in her floury apron she looked like a mother. "Greg, it's time for you to practice."

"Oh, no."

"Oh, yes. If you do a good job, you can play your piece for Annette after supper."

"And for Ox. See ya later, Ox."

"Not if I see you first."

"Ox, huh?" Annette said when they got upstairs.

Katie groaned.

"Oksanna's not so bad. It's kind of nice."

"My grandmother's name. Gidú told me once he hoped I'd use it someday when I was older. I would now, if it

57

didn't turn into Ox. It's my first name, actually. But I made my parents leave it off the forms for St. John's, so I'd officially be Katherine. If one person calls you Ox on the first day, you can be Ox till you graduate."

"Like Dawn and her 'little Injun' routine. Did I tell you she calls me that?"

"That's awful."

"There's not much I can do about it."

"I hate it when people do stuff like that." Katie gestured toward heaven. "People are such jerks! Come on, let me show you some albums."

Supper was pot roast and noodles. Mr. and Mrs. Danbor, calling each other Anatole and Ruth, exchanged news from work and discussed weekend plans. Gidú was there, too, a tall, thin man, stooped and faded. Katie whispered that he usually ate dinner with them though he lived in his own house. After supper, Greg performed his piano piece.

"Now can I watch TV?" he said.

"Remember, young man—one hour and one hour only," said Mr. Danbor. He had sharp eyes above half-moon glasses that perched on his nose.

"Yes, Father." Greg saluted before he went into the living room. Mr. Danbor winked at Annette and Katie.

Mrs. Danbor had a meeting to go to. Annette noticed how she and Mr. Danbor kissed before she left. Annette turned away from their embrace, but in an odd way she liked seeing it.

The people who were left sat around the dinner table, drinking tea.

"More trouble in Armenia, Dad," Mr. Danbor said to Gidú.

The old man grimaced, as if to say, What do you expect.

Mr. Danbor poured himself more tea and headed toward his study with pile of newspapers under his arm. "Sorry to disappear on you, folks," he said. "They've asked me to come up with an extra editorial by tomorrow. The Middle East. As if I knew what to say about that one."

Annette liked watching Gidú sip his tea. He had a peaceful face.

"You must come with Katie and see my garden," he told Annette. "And of course meet your grateful friend, Roger."

"I'd like to," said Annette. She was pleased that he knew who she was.

Katie gave Annette a thumbs-up sign. "He doesn't invite just anybody."

"Most young people bounce."

"Gidú," said Katie suddenly, "some kids at school are calling Annette names."

Annette hadn't realized Katie was worried about it.

The lift of Gidú's eyebrows said he was saddened but not at all surprised.

"You don't know what to do about it," Katie said. It was a statement, not a question.

"You can't change them," Gidú said, with a tiny emphasis on "them."

Katie looked disgusted. "A big help you are."

Annette did feel helped. His emphasis didn't put scorn on "them." She thought it meant she couldn't change other people, but she might change herself.

When Mr. Danbor emerged from his study to drive Gidú home, Katie and Annette cleared the table and loaded the dishwasher. After they'd kicked Greg out of the living room to go to bed, they watched some TV themselves, and then Katie walked Annette to the bus stop. While they were waiting, she said, "I haven't given up on a solution. I just haven't thought of anything yet."

"I won't tell about Ox," Annette said.

| ◆ |

The following Monday after school, Annette sat across from Katie on the floor of the student lounge, eating peanut-butter crackers with a carton of milk. Katie was dieting with a one-calorie soda.

"My dad says Indians invented lacrosse," Katie said. "Besides, if you make a team, you get out of gym. And a sport's a lot sexier than gym class. Hockey's a good fall game. The teams here are supposed to be first-rate."

"You sound like my mum," Annette said.

"Gimme a break."

"That's how she sometimes talks, is all. V.S.J."

Katie's face went blank, then lighted up. "Aha—the opposite extreme of N.N., which is Very St. John's."

"You got it. And I'm not sure I want to try out for anything."

Katie lightly thumped her fist on Annette's leg. "You told me you love to run. You beat me easy. I was dying, and you weren't even winded."

While Annette tried to figure out why she didn't want to try out, Muffy Anderson dashed into the lounge wearing a cheerleader outfit. She popped some coins into the soda machine, grabbed her soda, and dashed out again. "Hi, guys," she tossed over her shoulder as she left. Annette had realized Muffy *was* the kind of girl who was nice to everyone. Katie was not.

"Talk about V.S.J.," Katie said. "But Muffy's not a bad kid, you know? She sort of can't help it."

Finally Annette hooked some words. "Beating you wasn't the point. The reason to run is just to run, for no reason."

"But you try in your classes. Come on—you know you do."

Annette knew Katie was right. "Yeah," she said. Always the conflict.

"So are you going out for hockey or aren't you?"

Gym wasn't so bad now, since she was at last starting to have breasts, but it was usually something boring like aerobics, and indoors. Being outdoors was a joy.

"Okay," she said.

"Good-o," Katie said, grinning. "You and me against the V.S.J. world. I'll meet you at the tryouts tomorrow."

"You're going to try out, too?"

"With my incredible speed? No, I'm just coming as your cheerleader. Maybe I can borrow Muffy's pompons."

| ◆ |

The tryout turned out to be fun. A few of the others had never played before, either. Ms. Havens, wearing a plaid kilt, had them run short distances, fast, and then a mile, to see how they'd hold up. She gave them sticks and showed them how to pass, receive, and check. After a bit of practice, she had each girl dribble and pass, with her as a partner. Annette received the ball when Ms. Havens flicked it to her and she dribbled it without losing it.

"Now try to get the ball away from me," Ms. Havens said. Annette guarded Ms. Havens a little harder than she meant to.

"Good checking," Ms. Havens said.

"Way to go, Annette," Katie yelled from the sidelines.

Katie hung around while Annette changed. "I'll phone you up tonight," she said meaningfully.

When the phone rang, Mum answered. "Hi, Katie," she said. "Hope you can come by for supper here sometime soon. . . . Yes, she's here."

"Guess what happened while you were running the sprints!" Katie said. "Dawn was waiting with us to run next. 'Look at that little Injun go,' she says, real nasty."

Annette felt alien, dark, different. She thought she should be immune to Dawn's put-downs by now, but she wasn't. "I'm glad I didn't hear her."

"But that's not what I called to tell you," Katie rushed to explain. "Kevin Black—he's a junior who acts in all the plays—he was hanging around watching, too. He waited till Dawn ran out onto the field. Then he said loud enough for her and everyone to hear, 'Look at that bigot waddle.' Can you imagine anyone saying that to Dawn? A lot of kids laughed and Dawn turned red as a beet. She glared at Kevin and he gave her a little two-finger wave. I think Kevin must like you, Annette."

"But I don't even know him."

"That doesn't matter."

"He probably just thinks I'm a noble cause."

"You're being paranoid. He's not like that—he's really nice. And besides, he's hunky. Well, not hunky, exactly, but neat to look at. If you don't want him, you can pass him on to me."

Annette started to giggle. "Sure," she said.

Katie giggled, too. "Well, anyway, tomorrow Havens will post the names. I think you made the team. You looked just as good as most and better than some. You led the pack in the mile."

"We Indians are natural-born runners. Like blacks got rhythm."

Katie giggled some more. "That was a N.N. remark if I ever heard one."

"I'm allowed to make jokes," said Annette. "People who are N.N. aren't allowed to make them."

Mum gave her a funny look when she got off the phone. "What was your day like?" she asked. "Anything special at school?"

Annette didn't want to tell Mum about the tryouts or Dawn or Kevin. She'd work these things out for herself. "We're starting a big project in art," she said. "Where's that envelope of photographs?"

"Top drawer of the maple chest, I think. Did I tell you Peter's coming to dinner?"

"Again?"

Mum blushed. "It's only the second time. I thought I'd make a raspberry pie."

Annette took the big manila envelope into her room and spread the pictures out on her bed. She spent a long time gazing at scenes from home for the drawing she would begin tomorrow, a drawing Mr. Swanson wanted to be the basis for a woodcut. Again she wished she had a picture of Granmaw. But she didn't, and she didn't dare draw her without one. Besides, it wasn't the kind of thing Granmaw would like.

As she pored over the photographs, the drawing began to form in her mind. It would show a narrow, steep-sided harbor ringed with evergreens. The resin smell of the evergreens in the sun, rising out of them like mist. No wind. Quiet. How could a person draw quiet?

In the distance, under the same warm sun, a fishing

boat would rise and fall on the waves. The deep, cold green water, the salt air. Three small figures in the boat: Gino, Kiki, and her father. Mum had said he used to fish with Gino before he went to Vietnam. Annette had never really known him. But she missed him.

In three corners of the rectangular woodcut, she'd carve their faces. She remembered them, but she wanted the photographs to help her. Kiki was there squinting in the sun in the back row of their school picture from last year. It wasn't how he actually was, but it reminded her of the look of him. His energy. The intensity of his eyes. Something hungry. How could she show that Kiki was unsatisfied, incomplete? Perhaps she would make her lines incomplete. Perhaps part of his face would be missing.

Just before she and Annette had left for Victoria, Mum had taken a snapshot of Vera, Gino, and the babies in front of their house. Again, it wasn't a good picture— Gino's face was dark and partly obscured by Tom. But he was smiling his crooked smile. His dark hair partly hid his broad forehead. The picture she made of his face should say, I can do any job that needs to be done.

The picture of her father was the best in quality because Mum had made him go to a photographer before he left. "But he wouldn't let the man pose him in a leather chair inside his studio. He insisted that he take the pictures out of doors," Mum had told her. So her dad stood in front of a leafy hedge in a work shirt with the collar open and the sleeves rolled. His hands were thrust deep into the pockets of his corduroys. His chin was raised. His head was cocked slightly to one side. He smiled only enough to say, This is who I am, take it or leave it.

When Annette got into bed, she didn't know what to put in the fourth corner. But when she woke, the woodcut was in her mind, the images and the spirits behind them. The spirits fluttered gently, like butterflies warming themselves in the first sunlight. They stayed, waiting, while she went through the motions of breakfast and getting to school.

Katie was waiting for her by her locker. "You made it!" she said. "I already looked at the announcement board." She pounded Annette on the back and then gave her an enormous hug.

"Hey—I guess that's good."

"Of course it is, you dope."

They went, grinning, into chapel.

"Congratulations, Annette," squeaked Ms. Havens.

"I saw you made hockey," Muffy said.

Annette didn't hear much of chapel, not even the hymn, though she rose to her feet with the others, moved her lips, and sang the words. She gave thanks to the gods for the fleetness of foot that had won her a place on the hockey squad. Then, as she often did in chapel, she lost herself in the image of St. John with his mysterious bowl and serpent. Who was the person who had done that drawing, chosen those colors, placed those chips of glass?

After chapel, she drifted unaware through the crowded hallways, entered the art studio, and picked up her pencil. She would put a leaping salmon in the fourth corner. She had the magazine picture in her pocket, the one she had taken to Miss Doud's class. The salmon wanted her to draw it.

A noise in the distance distracted her. She heard her name and looked up to see Mr. Swanson.

"I said your name four times," he said. "The fourth time it got through."

"What?"

"It's first period, and you're not usually here. I wondered if you shouldn't be in some other class."

"Oh." She tried to pull herself away from where she was and be here with Mr. Swanson instead.

"What do you usually have after chapel?"

"I guess gym."

"And then?"

"Math."

"And then?"

"English." She remembered the pink slip and detention. Mr. Swanson was making sense to her now. "Oh, boy," she said. "I guess I'm in trouble."

Mr. Swanson laughed and wrote out a late pass. "Give this to Miss Havens. Then go to math and English. I'll see you after lunch at our usual time." He gestured toward the salmon and her drawing. "We'll all be here."

◇ 10 ◇

Annette returned to her drawing after lunch. At the end of the class, Mr. Swanson said, "I'm usually here after school, until five or so. You're welcome to come and work. There might be a few other students around, too."

"I'll come before hockey."

On rainy afternoons sometimes scrimmages or games were cancelled. Those days there was time to sink deeply into every part of the woodcut—the faces, the harbor, the process of doing it. The lines came alive. The tools did what she wished.

After the weekend, it was harder to feel connected to her artwork. Mr. Swanson watched her trying to get started one Monday morning. "I come in on Saturday mornings," he said. "I'm working on my own stuff, getting ready for a show, and I don't talk to anyone. But the room's open until noon or so, if you want to work. Those same kids you see after school come in, seniors getting portfolios together."

"I hadn't really noticed them," said Annette.

Mr. Swanson smiled. "I know."

| ♦ |

But she had started to notice the other Indian kid from over west, Joe Martin. He wasn't just in Miss Doud's class. He was in math and English, too. One day in late November, Joe came late to Mrs. Greenwood's class, again. He didn't have his homework, again.

"What is your explanation, Joseph?" Mrs. Greenwood demanded.

Joe just stood there with a face that was neither here nor there. Then, Annette saw Joe pull himself into the situation and politely smile, because he thought Mrs. Greenwood wanted him to.

"This is no laughing matter," she snapped. "I'll thank you to wipe that smirk off your face." Mrs. Greenwood put her hands on her hips and got red in the face. Her gray snail hairdo trembled. The glasses she wore on a chain around her neck glittered with rage. Even her earrings looked angry.

"You'll never make it past Christmas," she said. "We sweat blood over you people all during the fall, trying to teach you to manage your time and to analyze facts, but you can't learn. You are incapable of it. You think you can show up when you please and do your work when you feel like it—but you can't. Not at St. John's. Then, after we've poured months of effort into you, you'll go back to your village at the holidays and never return. I can't seem to get the headmaster to realize—we shouldn't *take* native students. It's a waste of our energies, and our other students, who can profit from our attention, suffer as a result. I give up on you, Joe. I just don't know why I bother."

Annette was angry for Joe and for herself. It was as though Mrs. Greenwood were yelling at both of them.

| ◆ |

The St. John's outfit changed from a wool blazer to a wool blazer with a long red-and-white-striped scarf, draped this way and that, its fringes flying. Hockey had only one more game. Some Cricket Club kids chattered about gowns for their New Year's Day ball, and in chapel one day the headmaster read the first installment of *A Christmas Carol*.

Mum only got Christmas and New Year's Day off, and both were Wednesdays.

"It's because I'm still the new girl in town."

"I'd like to go up home for most of the vacation," Annette said. "I've been thinking about it ever since September."

Mum looked a little wistful. "I'll miss you," she said. "But I think you should go. We can have our Christmas early. What would you think of inviting Peter, too?"

"If you want."

"I think he'd enjoy it."

"I thought you didn't like doctors."

"He's one of the decent sort. But we don't have to have him if you'd rather not."

Annette had noticed how often Peter Harris came into Mum's conversation these days. He'd given her a book of poems for her birthday.

"I'd rather have just us."

69

They exchanged gifts after supper on Annette's last day of school. Mum made roast beef and set fire to some hot brandy she poured over a plum pudding. The flames danced blue around the dish and then went out, leaving a fruity smell. Annette liked the cold hard sauce together with the hot pudding.

She gave Mum the first print of her woodcut.

"It's wonderful," Mum said. "I knew you were good, but I guess I didn't know you were *this* good."

Mum gave Annette her present with a big apology. "It won't be your best gift," she said. "Just something useful."

"I bet it's another watch."

It was. "Pretty boring, huh?" said Mum.

Annette had broken one and lost another. "I guess I need it."

"I'll think of something fun and mail it to Granmaw's," Mum said. "Your gift is my very best one. Peter's been asking me what I want for Christmas. Now I know what I'll tell him—I want the perfect frame and mat for this. He dropped this box off, by the way."

Annette saw it had her name on it. "What did he do that for?"

"Annette! It's Christmas! Maybe he just felt like giving you something."

The gold metallic box was too shiny and the ribbon was too green. Inside was a long red-and-white-striped St. John's scarf.

"Oh, isn't that perfect!" Mum exclaimed. "I bet all the kids are wearing them."

Part of Annette wanted to dress like all the kids. Part of her wanted to tie her hair back with a leather thong.

"You never had boyfriends up home," she said.

Mum opened her eyes wide and raised her eyebrows. "I didn't want to, then. And there wasn't anybody around. Don't you like Peter?"

"He's okay." She went to pack for her trip. She left the red-and-white-striped scarf on her dresser in its shiny gold box.

| ◆ |

When the driver announced that the bus for Ucluelet and Port West was loading, Annette kissed Mum good-bye, joined the queue, and climbed on board. She put her little canvas suitcase in the overhead rack and took a window seat.

It was very early in the morning. Stars still shone in the dark sky. Annette thought Victoria stars looked weak and watery compared to the stars at home—and there weren't nearly as many. At home, the sky was often overcast. But when it was clear, it was unspoiled by city lights, and the stars clustered thick as berries.

"I love you," Mum mouthed through the thick window glass.

"I love you, too," Annette replied.

As the bus filled up in the dark morning, she glanced out the window and noticed with alarm that Joe Martin was struggling toward the bus with four big pieces of luggage. She should have realized he'd be traveling to Ucluelet, too. She just hoped he wouldn't sit with her, taking up three quarters of the seat space and being bad company for a whole long day of travel. A big fat problem.

71

Other seats remained empty. Maybe she'd be lucky. Most of Joe's suitcases went in the storage hatch under the bus. He only had one bag in his hand when he came down the aisle.

"Hi, Joe," she said, feeling she should at least be polite. At school, he barely nodded to her. Today, though, he paused by her seat to talk.

"Hey, Annette," he said. "Free at last, huh? Getting away, at last? I'm going to forget that place so quick. Mrs. Greenwood—I'm going to forget her first of all."

"It'll be nice to be home," Annette agreed.

"Nice!" said Joe. "Nice! It'll be fantastic. The best. The greatest." He gave her a dismissive nod and went on toward the middle of the bus, where, to Annette's relief, he took the last empty double seat.

The bus driver started the engine and revved the motor, getting ready to pull out.

Out the bus window now, Annette could see that the sun was rising, making a brightness behind the cover of clouds. Granmaw told time by the sun. When her bladder was full and daylight touched her eyelids, it was time to wake up. Not like Katie, who had a digital clock radio with snooze control.

Just as the driver was putting the bus in gear and starting to back out of the diagonal slot, one more passenger came bursting from the station and dashing up to the bus door, banging on it with a mittened hand. A person who was late! Whoever it was, Annette felt sympathy for this passenger, who perhaps refused to use an alarm clock and who had waited for the light.

The driver, who seemed to be a jolly sort, cranked open the door and let the latecomer in. Annette was startled to see who it was—the tall boy whose blond hair fell over his

72

forehead like a shining curtain of water, the boy at the gate from the very first day of school. He smiled when he saw her. He gave the driver his ticket, came down the aisle, and sat next to her.

"Hi, Annette," he said after he'd arranged his coat on the rack and his knapsack between his feet. "I know you from school. I'm Kevin Black."

◆ 11 ◆

Annette felt shy, but she said hi to Kevin. He could have sat anywhere, she thought. Why'd he sit next to me? Still, she was pleased, and curious about him. His blond hair made her think of Mum.

"Heading for home?"

"Ucluelet," she said. Port West was even farther, but nobody had ever heard of it. She'd learned in her fall term at school that people were happier if she said she was from Ucluelet.

"I'm going to my parents' house in Nanaimo. I've been living with some friends of theirs so I could attend St. John's. They're nice people, but I can't wait to be home."

There was a long pause. Kevin patted his shirt pocket, where Annette could see a pack of cigarettes. Then he glanced at the Smoking in Last Three Rows Only sign, then looked out the window, then gave a big sigh. He brushed the hair off his forehead. He looked at Annette and smiled, as though he felt nervous and it was her turn to talk.

She wanted to know Kevin better, but at home people didn't ask questions or explain their lives. They waited. They observed. They noticed. They took the other person in through their pores. She couldn't think of anything to say until she came back to the friendly feeling she'd had toward the person who came to the bus door late.

"The bus almost left without you," she said.

Kevin laughed. "That was dumb. I was inside the station, reading. I guess they announced the departure, but I never even heard it. The woman who sells the tickets came over and nudged me or I'd still be there."

He showed Annette the book—*Never Cry Wolf* by Farley Mowat. "My body was in the Victoria bus station, but the rest of me was in the Arctic Circle, with the wolves. Lost."

"That happens to me all the time," said Annette softly. "I get watching the wasps and then I'm late to English and Mrs. Greenwood yells and gives me a pink slip."

Kevin turned to face her. "I bet I know the ones you mean. Out under the eaves at the end of the hall. In the fall they got busy if it was warm."

Annette nodded.

"I go there to sneak a cigarette. After lunch."

"I just go there and I get lost and then I'm late again."

"Lost," he said. "Not there. Out to lunch. Not paying attention. Asleep at the switch or off in a time warp. People don't like it when you go into a time warp, especially if you're reading an unassigned book. 'Kevin Black!'" he said in a good imitation of Mrs. Greenwood's voice and manner. "'Who gave you permission to sit in my class and read an *unassigned* book?!'"

Annette smiled. "You sound just like her. She makes me feel terrible. I don't like her."

"She's not so bad. She's just a lady who's tired of teaching and trying to hang on for a couple more years till she can retire. Her husband's dead, so she's lonely. She never had any kids but her students, and now they don't like her as much as they used to."

"How do you know that?"

Kevin shrugged. "I just do. Her retirement is common knowledge—she even talks about how she can't wait till her last two years are up. I want to be an actor, and so I have to try to get inside people, see the world through their eyes. Even people that seem dumb or that I really can't stand. I have to understand their black rocks."

Annette thought about black rocks—rocks black with wetness down by the ocean, beautiful and shiny. Sometimes with gulls on them, sometimes with sun, sometimes with saltwater puddles on their tops reflecting the sky and clouds. Sometimes covered with mussels, or barnacles, sometimes with seals and seaweed. Frisky seals in the cold weather, sleepy seals on warm days. Rocks that were solid and went back to the beginning of time. Nobody could "own" a rock. Nobody could "have" a black rock. What did Kevin mean? She didn't like to ask.

"We have black rocks at home," she finally said, "down by the water. Big boulders and cliffs. Very beautiful."

He looked interested. His eyes were startlingly blue. "Ah," he said. "Black rocks by the ocean. Cliffs. That's not what I meant. I meant the small, jagged kind people carry in their hands to protect themselves. Parts of themselves that hurt, or that they don't like, so they turn them into ugly black rocks and use them for weapons. Black rocks is what my acting teacher calls them. Mr. Singleton, at

76

school. He's great. Not everybody's like Mrs. Green-wood."

"I have Miss Doud," said Annette proudly.

"You like her?" asked Kevin, apparently a bit surprised.

"Miss Doud is a black rock."

Kevin was silent a long time. In fact, Annette was afraid she'd said something wrong and spoiled the conversation, but he finally smiled. Then he laughed. "I get it!" he said. "*Your* kind of black rock. Good old Miss Doud! Who would've thought she was a cliff or a beautiful boulder? But do you see what I mean about the other kind, the small, ugly ones? The kind people throw at each other?"

Annette remembered Mrs. Greenwood's face when she was angry at Joe, her quivering hair, her earrings and glasses glittering like mica. She imagined Mrs. Green-wood with a small, jagged black rock in each hand. She had taken old age, fatigue, and loneliness and turned them into impatience and anger. She had taken her disap-pointments with her life and turned them into criticism of a student she couldn't reach and didn't understand. Her disappointments were her black rocks.

"I see," she said. "And I see what my small, ugly black rock is and what my large, beautiful black rock is. It's the same thing—being a Nootka, half, on my father's side. It makes me bad and mean sometimes. And sometimes it makes me happy and proud." It was what made her hate Dawn Mann and fail to give her report in Miss Doud's class. It was also what made her feel free and strong when she ran all afternoon on the hockey field or through the woods at home, or when she lost herself doing a woodcut of the fishing boat and her father's face.

Kevin's face filled with warmth and brightness.

"Wow," he said quietly. "I can't believe you said that,

Annette. That's the smartest thing I've heard anyone say all fall, even Mr. Singleton." Kevin patted his shirt pocket, as though reassuring himself.

"Gotta have a cigarette," he said. "This is an incredible conversation, but I'm going to die if I don't go and have a cigarette. Um—excuse me, okay?"

He jumped out of his seat and strode to the back of the bus. Before too many minutes had passed, the bus slowed, and the driver called out, "Nanaimo!" in a loud voice. Kevin hurried back down the aisle. He grabbed his coat and luggage and gave Annette a wave.

"See ya," he said. "Have a great vacation. I didn't realize we were so close to my stop. While we were talking, I kind of lost track of time. I guess we really are the same that way. A couple of aliens."

"Good-bye," Annette said. "You have a great vacation, too."

Watching him go, she felt their parting was a little abrupt, even though he turned to smile and wave at her through the window. Her time with Kevin—to observe and notice and absorb him through her pores—had hardly started and now suddenly it was done. It had no proper feeling of being over, no proper feeling of ending. It was like having to jump up and run at the sound of a bell. But at least she knew she liked him and she was pretty sure he had liked talking to her.

◇ 12 ◇

It was starting to rain, as it often did on the island, especially over west in winter. Annette didn't mind the gray, slanting drops. She gazed out the wet bus window anticipating her homecoming.

She had imagined the village and her life there many times on her daily bus ride to and from St. John's. She had comforted herself in that foreign setting with dreams of how wonderful it would be to return. Now the fir trees and mountains passing by the window seemed to bring her joyful reunion nearer.

Darkness fell and Annette dozed. When she woke, the bus was approaching Ucluelet, and she was surprised to see how poor it looked. The houses along the streets leading to the bus station were shabby and unpainted. Derelict cars decayed in muddy yards, like beached and rotting fish. Debris clung to the weed stalks and clogged the chain link fence in back of the grocery store. The body of a dead cat lay by the side of the road.

When the bus tires finally hissed off the wet asphalt and sloshed through the puddles in the unpaved parking lot, the station seemed small and dingy compared to the Victoria station. It was still raining. Annette was tired and stiff. Joe rushed past her in his hurry to get off.

"See you, Joe," Annette called out to him.

Though he was encumbered with luggage, Joe turned his wide body swiftly in the aisle.

"You'll never see me there again. I've had enough of that place." His broad face cracked in a grin and he looked alive—not half asleep or stupid—for the first time since she'd met him. "Farewell, Annette!" he said. In his voice rang a note of triumph.

Annette stayed aboard the nearly empty bus as it pulled out once again, this time heading for Port West, the end of the line. The bus stop was in front of the post office, not far from the clinic and her old apartment. But she was going to Granmaw's, and Granmaw had said she'd send somebody to meet her.

A strange man smoking a hand-rolled cigarette walked up to her. He was short and skinny, with dark, ragged hair and a white, curved scar over one eye like an extra eyebrow. He had a rolling gait, as though his legs weren't quite the same length, and the accosting way he smiled at her suggested that he wasn't from the village or had lived a long time away. It was a white, learned smile.

"You Annette?" he said.

"Yes."

"Granmaw asked me to pick you up. I live next door."

"Granmaw's got no near neighbors," said Annette, instantly wary despite her fatigue. She stepped back from him like a dog sniffing drugged meat in an outstretched hand.

The man laughed at her. "Come on, I won't bite you. I'm Tony. Iris and me put a government house next to your granmaw's trailer after our house burned down this fall. Iris knows your ma. She was Rosemary Anne Whitby before she married your dad. For some reason, Iris loves the sound of that name."

"All right, then," said Annette.

They ran through the dark and rain to an old Chevy with a faintly beery smell. A couple of Labatts Blue label empties lay on the floor of the passenger side and an opened can of Cinci Cream lager stood on the dash. Tony ground the starter four long times before the engine finally caught.

"How did your house burn?" Annette asked, trying to be friendly and make up for her earlier suspicion.

"Wood stove started it somehow. Must have been defective, or maybe I didn't install it right. At least we all got out okay, us and the kids. It's just as well. We needed to leave that place."

"Where did you live?"

Tony wiped moisture off the inside of the windshield with the side of his hand. "Up the coast, where I grew up. Beautiful, but you can only get there by plane or boat— the mountains cut us off. There's a big river that comes down. The planes that come in have to land on it. They buzz the river once to clear it, then make their landing. Iris said we should move to be closer to things because of the kids. She wrote your ma, the famous Rosemary Anne Whitby. Your ma got in touch with your granmaw. So I'm your neighbor now."

Annette found it hard to imagine Granmaw with near neighbors. Granmaw had always liked being on the edge of the settlement, connected but not too close. But it might be good for her to have people closer by now that she was getting older.

"So you been in the big city all this fall," Tony said. "Loaded with tourists, from what I hear. What do you think of it?"

"It's all right."

"Granmaw said that school gave you money to come. You must be pretty smart. You like it there?"

Annette decided not to tell Tony how unsmart St. John's sometimes found her. "It's okay," she said.

He took a swig from the can and offered it to her. When she shook her head, he said, "Aw, come on. You're home now—you can do what you want."

It doesn't feel like home yet, she thought, but was cheered by the idea of being with Granmaw soon.

"That's all right," Annette said. "I'm not much of a drinker."

She thought he might laugh at that, but all he said was, "Suit yourself. I couldn't get through the day without it. I can put away a coupla six-packs, maybe three, and not even notice." He turned toward her and gestured to the scar over his eye. "Bet you're wondering about that."

Annette hadn't wondered at all, but she felt Tony's need to have her ask and she gave in to it. "What is it?"

"War wound from Vietnam. My right foot, too. I only got eight toes now, an eight-toed sloth. That's why I walk funny."

"That's too bad," Annette said.

Tony glanced her way, and when she felt his eyes on her breasts, she turned her face to look out of the window. There wasn't much to see but darkness and rain. She went on staring out, avoiding his gaze. She turned back at the sound of a match striking and the scent of burning tobacco.

"Smoke?" he said, offering a hand-rolled out of his shirt pocket.

"No, thanks."

"So you're not much of a smoker, either," Tony said. "Such a good girl." The way he said it made her want to stick her tongue out at him, but she didn't. She didn't want to act like a kid.

"Okay, I'll have one." He handed her a cigarette and the matches and she managed to get it lighted. She knew enough from earlier experiments with Florence and Kiki not to inhale and choke and make a fool of herself. The smoke in her mouth tasted hot and bitter.

Tony gave her an amused glance. But he seemed mollified by her joining him. "You got a boyfriend, Annette?" he asked.

The space between them on the car seat seemed suddenly too small and she wanted to make it larger. She thought of Kevin, sneaking cigarettes out by the wasps' nest, breaking a strict school rule. He had defended her to Dawn. He liked their talk of black rocks on the bus.

"Yes," she heard herself saying. It wasn't quite a lie. He was a boy who was a friend.

"A white boy, I bet. Well, that's okay. I had a Vietnamese woman when I was over there. I used to see your dad over there, too. Not that we were big buddies or anything. We weren't in the same unit, but we got together a coupla times. We were the only Nootka around. He was a good guy, your dad."

"I barely remember him," Annette said, but she looked at Tony with new interest. He made her uncomfortable.

But it was neighborly of him to come and get her. And she couldn't help being drawn to him if he had known her dad.

He stopped in front of Granmaw's. Across the porch pillars hung a white banner with red letters. Welcome Home Annette! it said.

"Hey!" she said. "Look at that. Isn't that something." The thought that someone had gone to all that trouble for her made her feel happy down to her toes. "You didn't tell me there'd be a banner," she said to Tony.

He shrugged, exhaling smoke from his nostrils like a dragon. "Not my business to tell," he said.

Annette smiled at him. He was a Nootka after all.

"Who made it?" she asked.

"Your granmaw's sidekick, Mary Jones, the one that looks like a linebacker. She hung it up, with her husband, Gerald, that's built like a fireplug. He stood out in the yard saying it should be higher on the left, no, higher on the right. I tell you, it was comical. If he hadn't got that bear years ago, everybody would say she was the boss in that family."

Annette was touched that Mary had done the banner. She didn't think gruff old Mary had such a soft heart. Tony parked in the space between his new house and Granmaw's. He went with her into the trailer.

Annette was amazed at all the people who had gathered to greet her. Granmaw gave her the first hug, but all the others followed. Besides Mary and Gerald, there was Florence, looking womanly, and Kiki, looking tall. The person she didn't know, plump, with a slightly worried face, was Iris, Tony's wife, who introduced her two little boys, Aaron and Bub, pushing them at Annette until they finally peeked up at her and said hello. Tony leaned

84

against a wall, smoking and watching. He seemed proud of his kids.

The table was spread with some of Annette's favorite foods, smoked fish and wheat bread, as well as venison stew and a cobbler of the little wild plums Granmaw canned. When everyone had a plateful of food and was sitting quietly, eating and being glad to be together, Kiki asked, "So, Annette, do you like it down there?"

Annette's heart and mouth were full. Granmaw's house smelled right, of woodsmoke and coffee, the way it always had and always would. The look of the faces around her was the same as her own. They were dear, known faces, calling up memories. Mary Jones's enormous hands had showed her how to hem cuffs and sew on patches. Gerald had taught her how to spot clam spouts in the mud. She'd been through ten years of school with Florence and Kiki—mean Miss McLeod, boring Mrs. Andrews, challenging Mr. Feeney. They'd done plays, sung together, cooked mussels over fires on the beach. And Granmaw was part of everything in her life, like air.

When Annette could speak, she said, "It's all right. But this is home."

It wasn't until much later, after everyone had left, that Annette had another view of the group in Granmaw's trailer. She was just dropping off to sleep in her familiar, tiny room. She could hear the wind, and an occasional pop from the fire still burning in the wood stove. We connect just by being together, she thought. It's enough just to be.

Annette was not completely sure what she meant, but the words felt true. I'll tell Miss Doud, she thought. And she knew that St. John's had given her a new angle of vision. It had made its mark on her.

◇ 13 ◇

Annette spread two slices of wheat-bread toast with Cheez Whiz and bit into one hungrily. Inside Granmaw's trailer the blue enamel coffeepot perked gently on the wood stove. Strips of venison hung drying in a corner. On the kitchen counter sat a basket of onions and dried beans. Bits of dirt from Granmaw's garden clung to the onions. The room smelled fragrant and familiar, like no other place on earth.

"It sure is good to be here," Annette said.

Granmaw looked lively this morning, ready for conversation. It was an unusual mood for her.

"Bet your ma feeds you bacon and eggs," said Granmaw. "That's what she used to cook. Tomatoes. Fried bread."

Annette nodded. "I like that breakfast, too, but this is my favorite."

Granmaw took the coffee off the stove and poured it into a couple of mugs. Out the window Annette was surprised to see the Chevy she'd ridden home in last night. She wasn't wild about having Tony so near, where she was likely to run into him.

"Funny to see a car so close."

"Your ma knows Iris from before. Their kids are cute. People have to live somewhere."

Annette sipped Granmaw's strong black coffee, made creamy with condensed milk and sweet with sugar. She gave a contented sigh.

"Mum makes tea for breakfast," she said. "'Proper tea,' she says, in a scalded teapot."

Granmaw's rainbow eyes gave Annette a little flash of defiance and recognition. "English tea, like what most people drink around here. Not me. I decided, a long time ago, when I was about your age. My granmaw told me how it was. The Spanish came first, with guns and diseases. They shot us and made us sick and we died. We fought back. Our women made up to those armed Spanish guards. Got them to take off their armor. Then knifed them when they were busy humping."

"They really did that?"

"Sure. Our women fought side by side with their men. The conquistadores wanted to make slaves of us. The Spanish fought in the open, so we knew what we were fighting. Not like the English. They showed up later, after the tribe had nearly been wiped out. They wanted to finish us off with Jesus, sin, and tea."

"You mean the missionaries?"

Granmaw grunted an assent. "When I smell tea, I remember a long church service. Up front, that poor beggar nailed on his two sticks. Like a smoked fish. The missionary's wife had a face the color of a sow bug. She passed around little one-bite sandwiches. Dabs. A slice of flabby

87

cucumber. Not food. Just enough to keep you from starving. I decided I'd never go with that stuff. We went home and ate venison stew with beans and onions. I drink coffee like the Spanish. Strong, like them."

During morning chapel at St. John's, everyone was stiff and somber in the chilly chapel building. They stayed quiet in their seats while the headmaster talked, talked, talked about goodness, sin, mercy, and school spirit. Annette had learned to put up with it. She couldn't imagine Granmaw sitting in the chapel. She'd never wondered before what Granmaw believed or didn't believe.

"You go to church at Christmas, like everyone," said Annette.

"They got pretty music. I like the candles. I like to see everybody. Saw Mary and Gerald's grandson, Sam. Twenty now. A fine young man. Asks me where you are. I think maybe he's got his eye on you." She laughed slyly.

"Oh, Granmaw, don't be silly." Annette barely remembered Sam, except that summers he visited and had showed off to them, the little kids, by snapping a branch they couldn't break across his knee with a loud crack. He'd been too old to play with her, Florence, and Kiki. She hadn't thought about him in years.

"I said you were at St. John's school. He asked what made St. John a saint."

"I don't know." Annette felt a little foolish, to have been a whole term at St. John's Academy and have no idea. She'd never found out about the snake and the dish in the stained-glass window.

"You care what he did to become a saint?"

"Not a whole lot."

"Got himself killed some way. It doesn't matter that you

don't much care how it happened. So what. Nobody has to know what you think. You don't always have to tell people the truth. Not if they're going to mess it up and use it against you. They made me your godmother in the church, but nobody has to know I don't hold with sin and Jesus. I like to hear the children sing. But now you know why I don't drink tea. I don't tell it to everyone."

Granmaw settled back in her seat and closed her eyes. Annette knew she was not asleep but that after so much talk, she wouldn't say anything else for quite a while. She'd spoken enough to last a week.

Annette felt as though she'd just had ears attached to her head after years of being deaf. She'd heard Granmaw mutter about the conquistadores and the missionaries before. But she'd never really heard her. The conquistadores were in the past, and she was young, alive right now. She'd always been eager to get outdoors, away from chores and Granmaw's mutterings, to play with Florence and Kiki. Now what Granmaw had said fitted in with what she'd been learning down in Victoria with Miss Doud, out of library books. Looking at Granmaw's dark, wrinkled face, Annette realized that Granmaw was one of the women in those books. To protect themselves, sometimes the women refused to talk to anthropologists or told them lies. But sometimes they told the truth of their history, myths, and stories. Annette's two halves, which were so often at odds, came together into a whole.

She wanted to tell Granmaw about the tribe's Secret Societies she'd read about. One group admired dogs because they were smart, good workers, and loyal. Once a year, the Dog Society killed and roasted dogs. Eating the meat would give you the good qualities of dogs. If you had a dog you wanted to save, you had to petition the Dog

Society before their feast day. When Annette had told the anthro class about the Dog Society, Dawn Mann had understood the point. She said, "My father calls salads and vegetables 'rabbit food,' and he won't eat them. Maybe he doesn't want to be wimpy, like a rabbit."

Annette wondered if Granmaw knew about olachen butter and olachen ice cream, where fish oil from the olachen was used like fat in cow's milk. One book had described a Kwakiutl potlatch where the host tribe's lavish gifts included a whole dugout canoe filled with berries! Maybe I could be an anthropologist, Annette thought. I could teach people about people who are different from them, so they don't have to think those people are wrong.

Granmaw sat quiet as a lake. Annette put her mug and plate in the little enamel dishpan.

"I'm going over to Florence's," she said.

Granmaw did not open her eyes, but Annette knew she had heard. As she was putting on her jacket to leave, Granmaw spoke.

"Later I got more to tell you about our ways. Now that you're back and almost a woman. It's time you trained yourself. Learned to be strong for the test. We survive because our women are strong."

Test? Annette wanted to know more right away, but she also knew that when Granmaw said later, she meant later. But she left the trailer excited. Granmaw was treating her in a new way, talking to her like a grown-up instead of bossing her like a kid the way she used to do. Telling her about the Nootka women killing the guards while they were "humping," giving her a sly look and saying that Sam Jones had his eye on her. She wondered what the test was that Granmaw was talking about, and she wondered if she could pass it. Soon enough, Granmaw would tell her, when the time was ripe. With Granmaw, time had to ripen like a hard, green plum slowly growing pink and tasty. Ripening would not be hurried. You had to wait.

◈ 14 ◈

Annette knocked and Florence opened the door. She looked heavier and her hair was longer. She looked more like Vera.

"Hey," Florence said. "It's you."

Annette didn't say anything, just smiled, glad to be there.

"Come in," Florence said, acting like a hostess.

Annette took off her coat and said hello to Vera and the kids. Busy with some blocks, Tom didn't notice her. Wilma walked right over and grabbed onto her pants leg, then walked herself along the couch, supporting herself with one hand. She wasn't a baby anymore.

"Sit down, stranger," Vera said. "Looks like you've got a new green parka. Have some tea."

Annette sat.

"How's your mum?" asked Vera.

"Okay."

"How's school?"

"Okay."

"How's Victoria?"

"Okay."

Vera ruffled Annette's hair and laughed. "Nootka talk," she said. "I thought maybe they'd teach you to open up down there." She poured out two cups of tea and put on her coat.

"Since you girls can mind the babies," she said, "I'm going to run over to Mary's and sew some Christmas gifts. You can probably get more out of her, Florence."

"You look different," Florence said when Vera had gone.

Annette glanced down at her red St. John's sweatshirt. She'd had her hair cut in a short, perky way that was new to Florence, and she was taller and getting a figure on her.

"Some different," Annette said. She remembered Florence's letter. "Thanks for writing to me," she said.

"So you got my letter?"

Annette felt guilty. Florence had written it on the blue stationery.

"Yeah. I should have let you know and written back. There were things to tell. . . ." Annette gestured that there was more than could be said on a piece of paper.

"It's a hard school, huh?"

"It was like I'd moved to Mars. So many new people with strange ideas. Then I sort of got used to it. It's not so bad. Are things here pretty much the same?"

"I guess."

"That's good. I was afraid everything would change while I was gone."

"But different, too."

"So what are the new things?" Annette asked. "Besides Tony and Iris's house next to Granmaw's."

Wilma toddled over to Florence, and Florence picked her up and held her on her lap like a piece of protection. "I wrote you the main thing," she said. "Kiki's my boyfriend now. My serious boyfriend."

Annette felt jealous but mostly curious. "How long?"

"All fall. Ever since you went away."

"Does he still get his moods?"

"Sometimes. Not as bad, though. It seems to help him that we're together."

"Remember that time we went clamming and you got more than he did, how mad he got? Wouldn't speak to either of us on the way home, even though I got less? Stayed away from us the whole rest of the week."

"He's still moody. He can make me worried."

"Why?"

"He can't find a job, not even part-time, so he's always broke. And he drinks too much beer. He hitches over to that bar in Ucluelet where his mother works. They know him and they let him drink free, even though he can't handle it."

"This school I've been at doesn't let you drink anything. If they catch you with liquor, they kick you out."

That's them—what's that got to do with us? Florence's face said.

Nothing, Annette's face said. What she'd actually been thinking was that a rule like that could help Kiki. A dumb idea, since he was here, not there. And the kind of idea that used to get Florence mad and puzzled at her, because it seemed "white."

"I'd like to see Kiki," she said.

"There's a dance tonight, at the school."

94

Annette nodded that she would come. A couple of the babies began to howl.

"I got to feed them their bottles," Florence said. "That's something else that's changed. I don't mind taking care of them anymore, not even diapers. Not that I love changing diapers, but before I couldn't even do it. I even think it would be fun to have a baby of my own."

Annette was shocked.

"Do you think about that?" Florence asked.

"Someday, maybe, like when I'm thirty years old." Annette laughed, a little embarrassed. "I can't imagine it now. I want to finish school. If I make it through this year, I think I might even want to go to college."

"I would never wait till I'm thirty!" Florence sounded appalled.

The two girls stared at each other, miles apart.

"I guess I'll be on my way," said Annette.

When Annette got up to go, she felt as though her sweatshirt was too bright against the faded colors of the room. Florence looked sad. We used to be friends, Annette thought, but that was ninth grade and back when we were children. We're not children anymore. Maybe we're not friends, either.

"How long you here for?" Florence asked as Annette took her leave.

"They give us a whole month."

"See you at the dance."

The noise of the babies ended when the door shut. Annette walked away, replaying her own N.N. words. Nobody could "give" a person a month, or a minute, or a day—nobody owned time. But that's how she had described the vacation to Florence, almost insisting on the St. John's way. She felt she even had a different walk now,

95

more of a stride, less of a moving through the air that happened to be in front of her body. Maybe when she and Florence and Kiki were at the dance they would feel more as they used to with one another—young, silly, and happy, without cares, worries, or secrets. At ease inside their bodies, the village, and the world. But Annette was afraid it couldn't happen.

As she strode along, she decided to visit some of her old haunts instead of going straight back to Granmaw's. She was out of her blazer and oxfords, back into faded jeans and boots. She wanted to see her old world, even though it might be a world she couldn't return to. Katie popped reassuringly into her mind—Katie wouldn't be thinking about having a baby. In fact, it was Katie who had put the idea of college into her head. "Maybe we could go to the same place," Katie had said, as though it were natural that Annette might go.

Maybe she and Florence would reconnect at the dance. They used to have fun at dances, pairing up for polkas, line dances, and squares. Like running, dancing made Annette feel whole and happy, as though her spirit could sing to her body's music. Like running, it had no purpose except to be what it was. And it was something glorious. She and Florence had a special grip for swinging, where one arm went behind your back for better leverage. With that grip, you could really swing your partner hard. In the meantime, she'd walk down to the school, just to see how it looked. See the woods, smell the ocean, enjoy the fog.

The school looked so small Annette thought it had shrunk, like a wool sweater you put in hot water by mistake. There was a wreath of grapevine and ribbon on the door and a poster announcing the dance that night at eight P.M.

The school door wasn't locked, so she went in.

The whole place had gotten tiny. The drinking fountain outside the first-grade room came up to her knees. The desks inside the room looked like furniture made for dolls. She walked down the hall feeling large and noisy in her boots and parka. The light was on in Mr. Feeney's office and the door was open.

"Annette!" said Mr. Feeney, jumping up and giving her a hug. She was astonished. Mr. Feeney never touched any of the students—ever.

"Hello, Mr. Feeney," she said shyly, but looking him in the eye. He looked a little embarrassed, as though he'd been caught off guard and done something very nice but now wanted to forget it.

"Sit down," he said. "I was just clearing up a few odds and ends, but they can wait. I'm off to Vancouver this afternoon for the holidays, so I'm glad to see you before I go. Tell me all about St. John's."

"It's okay," Annette said. She remembered how he loved his trips to Vancouver. For the first time, she wondered why he taught school here, far away from the city. She noticed what an undersized man he was, with thinner wrists and skimpier hair than she had observed before. Like the first-grade furniture, he seemed to have shrunk, now that he wasn't her teacher anymore.

"You like it? It's a grand old place, isn't it, and such wonderful facilities. A strong faculty. A marvelous tradition."

Annette nodded.

"You're doing all right in your courses?"

"I guess."

Mr. Feeney smiled—she supposed because of the vagueness of her answer. "What did your term report say?"

"It hasn't come yet. We just had exams before we left for the holidays."

"Well, what do you anticipate? Realistically? Based on your grades so far?"

Mr. Feeney had his brisk, probe-into-the-future look about him. Annette felt herself retreating from that look, as she had in the old days in his classroom. But recently she'd practiced prediction with her math teacher, Mr. Hicks. An educated guess, Mr. Hicks would have called it, insisting that she look at the whole shape of a math problem and estimate an answer. Mr. Hicks was always forcing her out of the present into the future, just the way Miss Doud was always forcing her out of the present and into the past.

"Not so good in English and math, though better than at midterm when I got D's. C's, maybe. The final exams weren't as hard as I thought they'd be."

Mr. Feeney's face was carefully controlled. "And your other subjects?"

"A in gym. I already know about that. A in art. That's a full-credit course and I already know that grade, too."

Mr. Feeney's eyes looked pleased. "Well, of course," he said. "You're an artist, among other things. Any others?"

"Just anthropology. I don't care what I get. I like it. The grade doesn't matter."

"Of course it matters," said Mr. Feeney, as though he were talking to a grown-up. "I went over the terms of your scholarship pretty carefully. In order to keep it, I know St. John's expects you to have an academic average of B by the end of your first year. If you get two C's, you need another A if you want a B average for this term. Gym doesn't count, you know."

Annette thought. A was "excellent." B was "good." Anthropology was both excellent and good, as far as she was concerned. "It could be a B," she said. "Or it could be an A."

"We'll hope for an A, then," said Mr. Feeney. "And it will be important for you to pull up those other two grades."

Annette wanted to stare at her boots, but she made herself look back at Mr. Feeney. Like Granmaw, he was talking to her in a new way, as though she were more of an equal and less of a kid.

"Tell me about your mother," said Mr. Feeney. "Is she liking Victoria? And her job?"

"Pretty much. She's making a lot more money. But then, we have to spend a lot more down there."

"And you've made some friends at school?"

Katie and Kevin. "Yes, a few," said Annette.

"You don't have to have everyone like you," said Mr. Feeney gently. "In fact, I wouldn't quite trust a person who was busy trying to get everyone to like him. A few good friends is all you need. I hope you'll consider me a friend, now that I'm not your teacher anymore. It's a treat to see you, Annette. The school hasn't been the same without you."

"I haven't been the same, either," said Annette. "I've missed being here." But she realized, looking around his bare little office, that much as she had missed it, she wouldn't want to come back.

"You have a special burden because of your special

heritage. But it can be a special opportunity, too. You just have to do something that's almost impossible—keep both parts of your heritage alive in your heart."

Again, Mr. Feeney looked a bit pink in the cheeks, as he had when he had hugged her hello. This was a side of him that he had not shown to her before in such an open way. Before, he had been proud of her, but mostly he just pushed her, to do more, to do better, to do well on the qualifying exams. She had resented it sometimes, because he didn't pressure any of the other kids the way he kept after her. Now she understood.

"Thank you for working so hard on me," she said.

"Thank you for thanking me. It was a pleasure," said Mr. Feeney. He walked her to the front door and shook her hand. When she looked back, on her way to visit the dock, he was still there, looking at her, and he waved.

| ◆ |

When she returned that evening, the poster on the school door still said 8:00 P.M. Annette's Christmas watch from Mum said the same. Yet the school was dark and the door was locked. No sign of a party or preparations for a dance.

Standing on the steps alone—washed, combed, dressed, and ready—Annette knew she really had become a stranger. She'd acted on St. John's time here at home, where it didn't fit. She felt odd, as strange as she had in front of Miss Doud's class when she couldn't give her report. What was happening to her?

Confused, and not wanting to sit on the school steps alone, she walked down to the deserted dock, just to have something to do. To kill time, as she'd heard Katie once say, when she was waiting in the hallway at school for her mother to pick her up. "Hi, Katie," she'd said. "Hi, An-

100

nette," Katie had replied. "It sure is boring here, just killing time." As though time were something a person could destroy, or would want to put to death. Yet here Annette was, doing it, in a way. Feeling embarrassed to be the first one at the dark, empty school. Not wanting anyone to discover her there, because then they'd know that she'd turned into a stranger.

At the dock, she stepped aboard Gino's boat, where women were not allowed. The cabin was unlocked, but she preferred sitting on the deck. She liked the strong smells of fish, rope, gasoline, and tar. The lift and drop of the swell soothed her. She felt as though she were sitting inside her woodcut, rocking quietly and endlessly, in the narrow harbor sheltered by tall rocks and fir trees.

When it occurred to her to leave the boat, the school lights shone through the dark. The door opened and shut, releasing a burst of "Beer Barrel Polka." Annette moved, neither fast nor slow, toward the porch light's pale yellow glow. She felt calm inside herself again. Perhaps she should be an artist, where she could be both inside her life and observe it at the same time. Perhaps that would be better than being an anthropologist. She didn't know. Her life seemed to be changing in all of its aspects, her body, her mind, the way people treated her—everything.

Right now she just wanted to have fun. She wanted to dance.

101

◆ 15 ◆

Music filled the small auditorium. Dancers whirled past, elbows cocked in red flannel, knees busy in jeans. Paper chains and gold stars, smudged with small fingerprints, festooned the windows. Faded maroon curtains—Annette remembered their musty smell—framed the pint-sized stage. HAPPY ran down one side in pinned-on red and green letters, and CHRISTMAS down the other. Voices, high and low, young and old, sang along with the record, "We'll have a barrel of fun."

The refreshment table stood on the stage, to leave more room for dancing. Annette perched on the stage edge, catching the scent of smoked fish. She waved as Vera and Gino polkaed past. At the opposite end of the room, Tony smoked and propped up the wall. A tall young man stood behind Gerald's and Mary's chairs. He had Mary's linebacker build and Gerald's face with its strong forehead and nose. Must be their grandson, Sam, Annette thought—she hadn't seen him in quite a while. He seemed to look at her with special interest. She smiled, just being friendly.

The beat was making her tap her foot, and when she spotted Florence and Kiki, who grinned and kept on dancing, Annette began to wonder who she might dance with. Some of the boys from school weren't around anymore, and there weren't that many to begin with. Kevin Black—that was who she wanted to dance with, but of course he wasn't here. On this dance floor he'd be too tall, too sharp featured, too pale, and much too blond. Annette remembered what Mum had said about coming to Port West as a young nurse and meeting Annette's father. "I certainly stood out," she said. "Everybody knew who I was."

When the polka came to a stamping finish, someone put on a slow dance. Someone else turned down the lights. Annette saw the two separate shapes of Kiki and Florence become one shape. Kiki was taller and more broad shouldered now. His black hair was cut short on the sides and long in back. He held Florence as if his life depended on her. Florence, in the dim light, gave herself up to being held. So they *were* lovers.

Tony appeared out of the shadows at her side.

"Dance, neighbor?" he said.

"I don't know," said Annette doubtfully. She'd agreed to do some baby-sitting for his and Iris's kids while she was home. She felt funny about dancing with him.

"Oh, come on," said Tony. "Iris'll keep an eye on me." With his chin, he indicated Iris chatting on the sidelines, holding Aaron by the hand and Bub on her lap.

"Okay," Annette said. She put her hands on Tony's shoulders, keeping a careful space between her body and his, and began to sway to the music.

103

"Your friends make a romantic couple," Tony said. "I seen you looking."

"I guess they are."

"They don't make no secret of it."

"Why should they?" Annette said quickly, wanting to defend them.

Tony's laugh smelled of cigarettes and beer. "No reason at all. They're young, but they're not that young. Kiki's near seventeen, I hear, and out of school now. It grows you up fast, being out of school. Staying in school keeps you like a little kid."

Annette made the space between them a little wider, and Tony laughed again.

"Now, don't get mad. We're supposed to be enjoying this dance. You looked like you wanted to be a romantic couple, too. That's why I asked you."

It was unsettling that Tony seemed to read her mind. Annette kept her eyes away from his face. At the last chorus, Tony moved his hands from her waist and pulled her against his thighs, belly, and chest. Her chin was suddenly resting on the soft flannel shirt covering his shoulder.

"You just pretend like you're with that boy in Victoria," he said quietly in her ear. "Let yourself go." As the music ended, he slid his hands down her sides and gave her hips an approving little squeeze. Then he released her, with a bow, and went back to stand near Iris as though nothing had happened.

Annette moved, with as much nonchalance as she could muster, to the girls' bathroom, to get control of her ruffled feelings. She was upset at the way Tony had touched her. He shouldn't have done it. She was also bothered that her body had found it exciting. When she saw her face in the mirror, her greenish hazel eyes looked larger than usual, and she thought, with surprise, Who's that pretty girl? That girl didn't used to be pretty.

Florence came in and leaned into the mirror to fluff up her bangs.

"My hair looks terrible," she said. "Taking care of the babies, I didn't have time to wash it. I love your haircut."

"Thanks," said Annette. Annette liked it, too. It had been Mum's idea. Annette wished Mum were here right now. Just knowing Mum was in the apartment over the clinic would have made her feel better.

"Having a good time? I wish this dumb old mirror weren't so small."

"Actually, I'm feeling kind of sick. I don't think I'm going to stay."

"But it's just started. You shouldn't go so soon. I got Kiki to say he'd dance with you."

"You didn't have to do that."

"Well, I wanted to. There's not many boys around tonight. It's no good coming to a dance and not dancing, or getting stuck with some older guy who's married."

Annette didn't want to go back out on the dance floor where Tony would be watching her with his mind-reading eyes. Now that she'd lied to Florence about feeling ill, she really began to feel a little strange.

"I need some air," she said. "Maybe I'm getting that flu that's going around. Your ma said the babies were all having it."

"I'll see you, then," Florence said.

"See you."

Annette pulled on her new green parka and started walking home. The night was dark and overcast. The vacation stretched out ahead of her, long and lonely. She wished she'd stayed in Victoria.

At least the glow in Granmaw's window meant she was still up. She had a hot fire burning in the wood stove and her hands wrapped around a steaming mug. Annette found the room stifling, but she knew Granmaw's old bones needed the heat.

"Sit," Granmaw said.

It was a pleasure to obey. Annette stripped down to her T-shirt, jeans, and bare feet before taking her place at the table. The air in the room was close. The kerosene lamp burned raggedly, sending shadows leaping on the wall.

Granmaw poured a second cup out of the pot. "Drink," she said. "Get the poison out."

How could Granmaw know? Maybe she just meant poison in a general way, not what had happened at the dance. The drink, neither coffee nor tea, was bitter and hot.

"In the old days, girls your age got initiated into the tribe. So they could be strong women to bear and raise the children. Training. A test—the ocean swim. Out in a boat. Jump in and swim to shore. So far away you couldn't see it. Getting ready, we used to sweat. Sweat, run, sweat, run."

The bitter drink, the heat, the flaring lamp and dark shadows told Annette to listen. Granmaw was telling her something she needed to know. Granmaw had often muttered about the "old days," but in the past Annette had never paid much attention. She'd run off with her friends. Tonight she understood that the *we* who sweated, ran, and swam might be Granmaw and her girlfriends—or Nootka women back at the faraway beginning.

Eventually Granmaw spoke again. Her voice had the slow, steady rhythm of falling waterdrops. "We ran on the beach, forward and backward. Ran without kicking up sand. Practiced the running. Practiced for the swim.

"When your woman's blood came, you went to the spe-

106

cial house. It soaked into the moss, going back to the earth. After, they'd take you out in the boat. You'd jump naked into the ocean."

Annette felt the shock of the cold, deep water, the plunge down, the slow rise to the surface.

"You'd start your swim feeling strong. Before you finished, you were close to dying. That was what you had to know. Death was all around. When its icy arms choked around your neck, you fought it off. You kept on, even after you couldn't move your arms or legs. Couldn't breathe. The struggle went on and on. Then the sand was under your feet. You staggered up the shore, half alive. The women put the robe on you. Gathered around. Brought you food. You were one of them."

Granmaw's rainbow eyes were so focused on the past that they no longer saw her, but Annette felt that every word was meant for her.

There was no special house anymore, with moss to receive her woman's blood. It was too cold to swim, and there was no "they" to take her out in a boat and greet her at the shore. But if she could not swim, she could run. She could sweat and train. She could run—a testing, ritual run. Farther than she had ever run before.

"I want to do that," Annette said. "I can't swim in winter, but I can run. You can tell me what I should do. Would you do that for me, Granmaw?"

The pause lasted so long Annette almost gave up hoping. Perhaps because she had English blood, she had no right to ask. Then Granmaw nodded her head yes.

Annette lowered her forehead to the table between her arms. She felt Granmaw's hand on her hair.

◇ 16 ◇

"Nine hundred and forty-two and nine hundred and forty-three."

"You in there?" Granmaw's voice came through the flimsy bedroom door."

Annette didn't answer. She had the kerosene heater turned up as high as it would go. Sweat was popping out on her naked body, the way it was supposed to, and she wanted to reach her goals—endurance, purity, and a thousand seconds, which was almost seventeen minutes. "Nine hundred and fifty-nine and nine hundred and sixty," she whispered.

Granmaw tried the handle. "You been sweating enough. I need some help!"

Annette heard her shuffle away and then the whack-bang of the agitator washing machine.

The day after the dance, Annette had started training for the Long Run. Each day she ran down to the beach to do leg lifts, push-ups, stretches, and bends. The weather was winter rainy, but not too cold, and the wind had not been bad. There was something invigorating about working out despite the weather, embracing whatever the gods sent. Today, for a change, the sky had cleared. Granmaw was out on her front porch doing the wash, and from her tone, laundry was more on her mind than initiations.

"Annette!"

The summons was serious. Annette reached one thousand and stood on wobbly legs. She wiped her skin dry with a towel and dressed, pulling on the hooded red sweat suit Mum had sent by mail for another Christmas present. It was now her Long Run suit. Without knowing what Annette was doing, Mum had sent the perfect gift. Apart from that, Christmas had come and gone without making much of an impression. Ever since Granmaw had said she'd help her prepare herself to become a Nootka woman, Annette's mind had been full of only one thing, getting ready.

After working up such a sweat, she was going to find the air chilly on that porch. She checked her face in the mirror, hoping to see some difference, but it was the same old face—broad at the temples, narrow at the chin, shiny brown hair now wet and stringy. No radiance in the green eyes over enduring the heat that made her heart pound, and the dryness that parched the membranes in her nose. No sign that poison had been driven from her body. Just a greasy face and fatigue.

Out on the porch, Annette started cranking. Granmaw fed the jeans and towels through the wringer. She wasn't angry. She had her long gray hair tied back by a strip of bandanna with a string of beads woven into its end, usually a sign of a talkative mood.

"Down at your school—you read 'bout the Bear Society?" Granmaw said.

"Sure."

"Tell what you read."

"The bear taught us to find all kinds of food, to be smart and brave, to have dignity, how to live. The only lesson the bear didn't teach was how to hibernate. Men killed the bear before they had learned that lesson."

"There's more," Granmaw said. "A bear fell in love with a woman. She went to live with it and learn its ways. She learned the secrets of its den and its long sleep. She slept next to the bear, wrapped in its warm fur, and since she was willing to learn and not afraid, the bear didn't hurt her."

The wicker basket was full. They went back inside to hang the clothes in the warm house, on lines strung along the trailer walls.

"You got it so hot. These'll dry fast."

"I turned the heater off," Annette said.

"You turn that heater off?"

"Yes."

It was quiet now with the washing machine silenced. "Sit," Granmaw ordered. Annette sat.

"There's more stories. A girl child was the first to come to this island. From a faraway place across the sea. In a little leather boat. Her sisters died during the trip, but their spirits survived and helped her. She found mussels to eat and built a shelter. Her boat had tools to make a fire. She burned her sisters' bodies on a driftwood pyre.

"When she grew up, she was lonely. She made a husband from the mucous of her own body. Their child began our race. It was a girl with green eyes. Like yours."

The eyes of an old soul.

They heard steps on the porch and a knock at the door. Tony stuck his head in.

"Howdy," he said. He held a paper bag containing his whiskey next to his leg. Not exactly hiding it. Not exactly not hiding it.

Annette nodded a hello.

Tony addressed his words to Granmaw out of respect. "Iris says can Annette come over to mind the kids this afternoon."

Annette nodded again. She'd been baby-sitting mornings as a regular thing, then training for her run in the afternoon. In fact, Granmaw told her that taking care of Iris's kids was something she had to do as part of her preparation. She liked Aaron and Bub, and so far she'd been able to manage being around Tony. Mostly he wasn't there. When he was, the worst he did was tease her by calling her honey. He'd swig straight from his bottle, not bothering to hide it the way he did around Granmaw. He said he called her honey because he liked to see her blush.

"Annette's our honey, isn't she?" he'd say to the kids, and laugh when they, not understanding the game, said that of course she was.

In spite of disgust with his drunkenness and anger at being teased, Annette felt the tug of that word. She thought her father might have called her honey, if he were still around. She wished he'd never gone to Vietnam. Fighting in somebody else's war was idiotic. He had no business to go off and get himself killed like that. She needed him. She thought she could remember him telling her a story about a bear and honey, and at breakfast, asking Mum to "Pass the honey, honey."

Tony shut the trailer door. Granmaw muttered, "Four generations."

Annette realized that a year ago she wouldn't have known or cared what Granmaw meant. Now she knew: It took four generations for people to undo the harm killing did to their spirits. While Annette's father was killed three weeks after he set foot in that tropical jungle, Tony served his full term and came back with his spirit hurt.

"Never has his hand off of that bottle," Granmaw muttered.

"You wish they weren't next door?"

"I didn't know about him before he came. So—you been sweating in that hot room?" Granmaw pinched Annette's arm. Her face, wrinkled and tan as a tobacco leaf, showed pleasure at the hardness of the muscle. "Been lifting rocks?"

"Just those heavy kids," Annette said. She was, in fact, learning a lot about babies from being around Iris. She knew it was good to push the baby out yourself and nurse it till it wanted to stop. Boy babies could squirt you when you were changing them, so watch out. Distracting Aaron from mischief worked better than punishing him. It was thrilling to hear Bub say his first word, "Kitty." But sometimes when Iris was late from work, Annette got to the ragged end of her rope and was ready to howl louder than the kids.

"A baby's important work." Granmaw pinned the last of the laundry to the line, a pair of her big, droopy underpants. "A tribe is a family."

"You got ready for the Long Swim with your friends?" Annette said.

Granmaw nodded.

"I was thinking," Annette said to Granmaw's back, "that maybe Florence . . ." Annette had been wanting a companion. Florence already knew a lot about babies. Though

112

the training was good alone, having someone to run with on these rainy afternoons would be even better. Every day she forced herself to go a bit farther, to build up strength. It was lonely work.

Granmaw shook her head. "Too late. Florence has already gone her way." She sat down heavily at the table and closed her eyes.

That afternoon Annette ran hard on the beach. The girl in her hide boat might have landed on this very beach. She had survived alone.

That night Annette's woman's blood came while she slept. In the morning Granmaw saw her scrubbing the stain from her pajamas. "How far was the swim?" Annette asked.

Granmaw only said, "Now, when you're ready, you can do your run."

Baby-sitting again at Iris's, Annette felt proud and happy but tired. When she lifted Bub to her shoulders, she felt a spurt of blood and worried that it would make a spot on her jeans. In the last half hour before Iris finally came, she was sick of the kids, ready to slap one and throw the other out the window. Instead, she sang one more song, played one more game. On the way back to Granmaw's she realized that was the answer to her question. The swim—the run—is farther than you thought you could go.

In the afternoon, training on the beach, she ran hard but lightly, trying not to kick up sand. You're a feather, a cloud, she told herself. You're a sea gull, scarcely leaving a track. But her feet landed heavily and the sand sprayed up like water. After five minutes, her lungs hurt and her legs ached. The whole thing seemed stupid.

Resting to get a stitch out of her side, she started a

letter to Katie in her head: I got my period today. And now I'm training for a marathon. Well, not a marathon exactly . . .

Katie had told her about a girl at St. John's whose father took the family out to a fancy restaurant when the girl became a woman. Katie had another friend whose mother slapped her across the face and warned her not to get herself knocked up.

Katie's own mother had fixed a special supper of Ukrainian dishes. Katie's grandfather had asked a blessing on "our family's young woman, Oksanna." So Katie had realized, after the dinner, that her mother had told the family and that in a quiet, private way, everyone was proud.

Annette started to plod up the steep road from the beach, hoping the stitch in her side was gone. What was the reason for enduring this pain and for trying to do the run?

The wind put its hand on her back. The sound of the waves below her made her feel as though she were running along the edge of the world. Finally, at the top, she saw the dead tree that held the eagles' nest. At school, a tree was photosynthesis and capillary action. Here, there was not much difference between a tree and a person because each contained a spirit. Granmaw would say some trees were better than some people. Like Hitler. A tall, kindly fir tree was better than he was. Any fir tree at all.

At school that fall, she'd been afraid she'd lose herself. Now she thought, If I can do this run, it will be something secret and sure to take back, a white stone to carry in my hand into the dark woods.

Annette turned and raced back down the road in giant strides. Then she turned and plodded up it again, going farther than she had before.

Granmaw seemed not to notice when she returned at last, the muscles in both calves twitching. But Granmaw saw. "Put on dry clothes. Sit. Drink this tea."

It was the same bitter, strangely satisfying brew she had offered after the dance. The heat from the wood stove made Annette's legs relax.

"Nobody can run without kicking up sand," Annette said.

Granmaw's shoulders shook with silent laughter. "Oh, yes," she said. Annette couldn't tell if she was agreeing, or saying, Oh, yes, you can. Or maybe both.

◇ **17** ◇

Tony lounged against the doorjamb while Annette fixed lunch for Aaron and Bub. Iris was going to be late from work—she had a doctor's appointment.

"It better not be another baby," she'd told Annette when Annette came over in the morning. The dark, desperate circles around Iris's eyes made Annette think of a caged raccoon.

"Saw you up the logging road," Tony said to Annette. The road up from the beach to the headland, where Annette had been working out, continued in a long, winding loop that ended at the east end of the village. She was using the first short section for her workouts. She planned to run its whole length as her test. Granmaw would not say how long it was, only that it was long enough. Needing to know, Annette had asked Gino. "Ten, maybe fifteen miles," he'd said.

Annette put the peanut-butter-and-jelly sandwiches on a plate. She carried three plastic cups of milk in her other

116

hand by the handles. She tried to stare Tony down at the doorway, but it didn't work. He grinned. She lowered her eyes. He wouldn't move aside for her to pass until she said, "Excuse me."

He followed her to the living room where she sat on the saggy couch to eat with the kids at the coffee table. The house didn't have a dining room, and the table in the kitchen was always covered with dishes and cooking pots. Tony leaned back against the wall, holding it up like he had at the dance. Annette knew he wouldn't sit down with her and the kids, and she'd never seen him eat. This was where he lived, but Iris was the wage earner and Tony didn't sit. He hovered.

"Guys used to log up there," he said. "That's what I used to do before I went to Nam. Spend all day with a chain saw and a mule. Mule snaked the logs out of the woods."

Annette imagined the resin smell, the sudden stillness of noon after the buzzing roar of the chain saw. She felt bad that his days of logging were apparently over. "It must have been nice," she said.

He leered, and she immediately regretted letting down her guard. "You got a logging road," he said, "you got a lotta dead ends, and some of 'em are lovers' lanes. A lotta babies get their starts in lovers' lanes. Lotta girls become women."

Annette stared at Tony, appalled at how he had read her mind but turned her vision ugly.

"Where I come from, a girl didn't go up the logging road unless she was ready," he said. "Ask anybody. Ask Iris how Aaron got his start."

Annette was grateful to hear Iris's old Chevy bumping along the muddy ruts of the road. It pulled up at the side of the house and in a minute Iris walked in, letting the door bang behind her. Her eyes were red and swollen.

"Annette, you can go home now," she said. "Tony, I've got to talk to you."

| • |

Annette kept training. She rubbed liniment into her sore muscles and tried, each day, to run farther before she quit. She gave up trying to get together with Florence. If Florence wasn't baby-sitting for her mother, she was occupied with Kiki. Annette was grateful to have the run to prepare for. It gave her something to do.

She phoned Mum to tell her about it.

"The sweat suit's perfect. When I put it on, I feel like it helps me."

"Don't overdo," Mum said. "You don't want to wear yourself out and wind up with mono."

"I'm careful," said Annette impatiently. "I got my period, too, Mum."

"Annette! That's wonderful! My baby is getting all grown up." Mum sounded as sad as she sounded happy. "Was everything okay? You felt all right?"

"Sure. I think Granmaw knew it would come. It's part of what I'm doing up here."

"I wish you weren't so far away while all these important things are happening. But that's a good place for them. Oh, I forgot to tell you that Katie called to get your address. She said her vacation was getting boring. She's going to write you a letter."

Annette smiled into the post office pay-phone receiver.

"Great. I'll be looking for it. I miss her, and you, Mum. And even some things about St. John's. I didn't think I would, but I do."

"I'm glad," said Mum. "Is Granmaw well?"

"She's the same."

Mum paused. "I'd be a little careful with Granmaw about the initiation. She may think she's wiping out your English blood and really turning you into a Nootka."

"But I *am* a Nootka."

"Half."

"An important half."

"I know that, baby. Your father would be proud that you're doing this. He was a fine runner and swimmer himself. A good hunter. Good with boats and fishing."

"I miss him, and I never really knew him." Annette paused. A restless wind stirred the tops of the fir trees outside the phone booth. "Why did he go to Vietnam?"

"It was a job he could get, when there weren't any others. He wanted to go to school after he got out, and the military would make that possible. He didn't think he could get an education any other way, and he thought it was a fair trade. He was so good with a gun and in the woods, I know he was sure he'd come back. It just didn't work out. Your picture of him is wonderful. It's hanging over the couch."

"Did you get it framed?"

"I asked Peter for a frame for Christmas, the way I told you I would, and it turns out he does matting and *makes* frames. He made one where the grain suggests the same grain you have in the print. The color of the mat is perfect."

"I didn't know he could do stuff like that."

"Deposit a dollar seventy-five for the next three minutes," the operator's voice cut in.

"I better hang up, Mum. I'll be seeing you soon. I'll call you."

"Run well and good luck," said Mum.

119

| ◆ |

The training went on, harder and longer. Just before it ended, Annette got Iris to take her along to town when Iris went for another doctor's appointment. Iris dropped Annette at the ball field surrounded by a quarter-mile track. The first mile took six minutes, the second eight, and the third ten. Three miles in twenty-four minutes wasn't bad, but her legs were jelly at the end. She forced herself to do one more, which made her jelly legs harden. She had only a few more days to toughen up.

Iris looked pale and shaky when she stopped to pick up Annette.

"You okay?" Annette asked.

"Fine," said Iris. She was shivering, though the day wasn't really cold and she was wearing a warm coat and a sweater. She hit all the potholes on the drive home and once veered almost into the ditch. Annette knew something bad had happened and didn't want to talk about it. But she wanted Iris to know she cared.

"If I had my license, I could drive," she said.

"Don't be in a hurry to grow up," Iris said bitterly. "Believe me, it's not worth it."

| ◆ |

The vacation was drawing to a close. Mum wrote about which bus to take and promised to be there to meet it. Annette read the letter at Granmaw's old, scarred table. "It'll be so good to have you home again," Mum wrote. Annette already knew she had two homes. Suddenly she realized that one day she'd have more than two. She'd be making herself more homes, all her life.

Usually Granmaw paid no mind to Annette's comings and goings. She dozed and liked to stay in the warm house. The day of the run, chilly as it was, she stood on the porch and watched Annette set out.

Annette walked to the beach, warmed up by stretching, and then slowly jogged up the logging road. She would have the hill to deal with first, the downhill to get her home. She wore her sweat suit but not her watch. She'd decided she didn't have to run fast, only to run well, only to finish. She ran lightly, trying not to kick up sand.

The logging road was overgrown in the center but passable along the two tracks. Running despite a familiar stitch in her side, Annette struggled uphill. Sweat mingled with liniment. At the top at last, she speeded up her pace along the flatland, shaking out the stitch, feeling her legs loosen and her breathing slow down. She figured she had made a good start on the course and was almost disappointed. The run seemed too easy.

Then the road passed into shadow, at the north side of the hill. When she worked out up here, she always turned back at this part. The woods were lonely, the logging trails were overgrown, the firs were dark and brooding. She felt her heart beating fast in her chest, with fear as well as effort. She was starting to hurt, not the pain of setting out but the pain of going on too long. Her legs seemed leaden and her whole body felt weak. What difference would it make if I walked for a while? she thought. No one would know.

The road started to rise again, and her body, right down to each individual cell, complained. She hadn't realized there was another hill. In the damp chill of the evergreen gloom, it was easy to feel sorry for herself. Her pace slowed to barely a jog. She was thirsty and her clothes were soaked with sweat. The road twisted and turned, sometimes rising sharply, sometimes gradually, but it never flattened. The ease of her run along the "summit" seemed a joke now. This road would never stop. It would only go up, and up, forever.

She was about to sag to the roadside when up ahead a bear emerged onto the road. It paused, seemed to glance at Annette, then looked back over its shoulder toward the woods. As though at a signal that the coast was clear, its cub trotted quietly across the road behind it. They both disappeared like spirits into the undergrowth. She knew the bears were real when she saw their paw prints struck into the soil. Her heart lifted, and she kept on up the hill.

Finally, after some miles had passed—she was becoming too worn out to guess how many—the hill crested and started steeply down in a series of hairpin turns. Her rubbery legs fought to keep her from slipping on the loose gravel. Breathing was easier, but sharp pains came in both knees as they braked to prevent her from plummeting down. She was so concentrated on her footing that she didn't see Iris's old Chevy parked in a turnout up ahead until she was nearly even with it.

Tony's arm was around her neck before she knew he was even there, and he was muttering ugly words into her ear. She smelled whiskey. She yanked to get free and he gripped her tightly.

"Come on, Annette," he said. "I told you not to come up here unless you was ready."

She was too tired to fight him. It would be such a relief to stop running that she almost didn't care what he did to her.

"Come on, honey," he said, an arm around her throat, dragging her toward the car. But she was *not* his "honey," and her sudden anger at that word made her lash back with a kick that got him in the groin. His grip loosened and she broke free. Then she really began to run.

She took enormous strides down the steep, rough road, scarcely able to pick out the sure footing as the uneven surface blurred by. Her knees could barely keep her from falling. She heard footsteps pounding after her and a hand grabbed at the hood of her jacket, but she kept running and soon the only panting she heard was her own.

She was afraid he'd come after her in the car. The trees were too thick to escape through and he could easily run her off the road. But she didn't think he wanted to kill her, and she knew he was drunk. She kept taking the hairpin turns, not hearing an engine. At the bottom, the road branched into a direct route to the village and one that seemed longer and less traveled. She chose the longer one, and as she rounded the first bend out of sight, she heard a car pass by on the other fork.

She kept on, and now, pounding along the flatland, mile after mile, she got her second wind. All at once, nothing hurt. She could run forever, up over the treetops, into the sky. She felt the presence of other women running with her, ghost women dressed in leather. Tony would not come back. If he did, she knew she could call upon their strength.

Tony did not return. Annette finished her run at the village outskirts and walked the road past the trailers to her home. According to her habit, Granmaw should have been inside fixing supper. Instead, she was sitting on the porch wrapped in a warm blanket. Mary Jones was with her. Annette stood in front of the old women, hands on her hips, exhausted, too tired to smile though there was a smile around her heart. She could go back to St. John's now. She had her white stone.

Granmaw looked at Annette for a long time, expressionless, silent. Then she got up and came down the steps. She put her blanket around Annette's shoulders.

"Kneel down," she said.

Annette knelt.

"Put your hands on the earth."

She flattened her hands against the ground. She felt Granmaw's hands on her head, pressing down till Annette's forehead touched the ground between her hands. She heard words, and though she no longer understood the language, she knew they were a prayer.

"Stand up."

Annette stood.

"Turn around."

Annette turned around and felt Granmaw's hands tying on the headband and beads. She faced Granmaw again when they were in place.

"Your secret name is Hai Nai Ya, the name Mowita gave her daughter. Mowita was a descendant of Copper Woman. Copper Woman descended from the first Nootka woman who came here in her leather boat. The name means the wise one, the one who knows. You are now a daughter of Copper Woman. You must look for wisdom. Listen to the earth and all that grows on the earth. Respect the gods of earth, sky, fire, and water. Learn to create and heal."

The ghost women who had run with Annette on the road stood close around her. She could feel their presence like a warmth.

"Go clean yourself. Then we will eat."

Granmaw went back up the steps. She and Mary went

into the trailer. Annette waited, in her new headband, with the blanket around her shoulders. She felt as though she could barely move her legs, as though to mount the steps were more than she could manage. As she waited, gathering strength, Miss Doud's words came to her: "Learning is not easy. It requires suffering, even pain. Anyone who tells you different is lying."

She looked at the dirt on her hands. She felt it gritty on her forehead. Wind sighed in the firs, tinged with the smell of woodsmoke from her neighbors' fires. Drops of mist, starting to blow in from the sea, settled on her face and hair like a blessing. She gathered herself together and climbed the steps.

When she had bathed and dressed, she sat, wearing her new headband, at the table with Granmaw and Mary. They had prepared the food for a ceremonial feast. The three women ate in silence. Granmaw and Mary looked at each other once. There was something about their exchanged glance that Annette didn't understand.

They finished their food. They sat over steaming cups of Granmaw's strange, bitter drink. "Now you can forget that English school," Granmaw said. "No more white poison."

"Now," said Mary Jones, "you can marry my grandson, Sam, and bear a Nootka child."

◈ 18 ◈

This was a time for silence. A time for the wisdom Granmaw had told her to seek. Annette lowered her eyes. She told her spirit to be still and ponder Granmaw's and Mary's words.

She could stay in Port West. She could live with Granmaw and learn to weave a basket so tightly it would hold water, to smoke fish so they neither rotted nor burned. She could go on taking care of Aaron and Bub—there would be no more trouble from Tony. She could watch the fog and be with trees and ocean every day. And Sam seemed okay. They would go around together and soon, even as soon as summer, her belly would swell with a child, her breasts would fill with milk. After the baby came, she would love it, care for it, teach it to continue the ways of the tribe. She had the strength to do that job. She had proved that to herself today. If she chose that path, she would be close to Florence again, for Florence was probably going to have a baby soon. Kiki would be her friend again, and Gino would help. Granmaw and Mary would guide her. Many feet had chosen that path. It was an honorable way.

If she returned to St. John's, she would have Mum.

Also the intrusion of Peter Harris. Katie. The challenge of Miss Doud. Clear light and turpentine in the art studio. The struggle of math and English. Lacrosse. The computer lab. The continuing problem of time. The sneers of Dawn Mann, the angry bafflement of Mrs. Greenwood. Instead of Sam, familiar in his looks and calm in his bearing, Kevin Black, with his blond waterfall of hair, his quick mind, clever tongue, and nervous hands. He was not peaceful. He was exciting. Did she want to be with Kevin? Would he soon find her dull because of her quiet Indian ways?

One of these lives she had witnessed for fifteen years. The other was new and led to an unknown future.

Mum had told her that her father had enlisted because of school. He had wanted a way into the world for himself. Surely he would have wanted it for her, too. She wanted it for herself. She didn't know if she could do it. But she wanted to try.

Annette lifted her eyes and spoke to Mary Jones first, thinking that her response to Mary would be easier. "I could marry Sam and soon bear a child," she said. "But I wouldn't be a wise woman if I did. I should be older and stronger first. I should be able to teach that child well and look after it with joy. If Sam got sick or died, I should be able to provide for it. As I am, I couldn't do that. I don't know enough. I'm not strong enough. I'm not ready to bear a child. Tony had that in mind for me today. He tried to catch me in the woods, but I got away. I'm not ready to belong to any man."

Then Annette spoke to Granmaw. "The English school has poison—it looks down on our people and their values. I feel it when I'm there. It makes me angry. It makes me want to run away and hide. But anger only makes the poison stronger and hiding makes life smaller. Hiding leads nowhere except to more hiding.

"In honoring my mothers, I must honor my own mother. The school is the school of her people. We have to understand their ways and make them work to our advantage. I can learn to do that in an English school.

"And I must honor my father. He didn't go to war because he wanted to kill people. He went because when he came back, he'd be able to go to school. So I think I shouldn't forget the English school. But as I take what it has to offer, I'll try to put it to good use. I'll remember what you taught me today."

Annette bent her head and prayed, not that Granmaw and Mary would understand, for their understanding was not within her power to bring about. Head lowered, eyes closed, she prayed only for the wisdom to accept whatever they had to tell her, whatever decision they made. She had put herself in their hands by undertaking the initiation. She could not defy them now.

For a long time, the three women sat in silence. The fire in the wood stove crackled. The kettle of water at the back of the stove made a low hum. A village dog howled, as though warning the forest animals to keep their distance.

"You did well not to let Tony catch you," Mary said at last.

Then Annette felt a hand upon her hair and knew that it was Granmaw's. "Always after the Long Swim, the new woman is asked hard questions. She doesn't know before what they will be, and she doesn't know the answers. Sometimes her questioners don't know either. Sometimes, nobody does. She must use her new strength to seek answers. Maybe we wanted you to say something else. But your answers are your own."

| ◆ |

A few days later, Annette got on the bus again to travel back to St. John's. She felt sad to go, sorry to leave home once again. She knew Granmaw was disappointed that she was going back, and she also knew that the next time she saw Florence, Florence would probably be a mother and the gap between them would have widened into a chasm. But she had talked to Mum on the phone again, and Mum had talked to Granmaw, and Annette knew that returning for the next term—and the next, and the next—was what she needed to do.

In her little suitcase she had her letter from Katie, or Oksanna, as she had decided to become. "I don't care if a few dumbbells call me Ox," Katie wrote. "In my mind, I'll spell their nickname Oks, and that will make it okay. Gidú is so happy. And my parents, too, though my father told me any name would be all right with him as long as it didn't begin with a *D*. He said he was not prepared to be a father to Dottie, Duffy, Dana, or Deanna Danbor. Or Dimples. 'I have my limits,' he said, 'and at Dimples Danbor I absolutely draw the line.'"

Annette enjoyed Katie's father's joke, though she rather liked Dana Danbor. Names were tricky. People didn't always get ones that suited them. But she felt honored to be Hai Nai Ya. She would tell Katie about her new name, but she would never use it at St. John's. It was a name for her first home.

Joe didn't board the bus in Ucluelet. She would miss him. She didn't like Joe, but she would miss him all the same.

She dozed to Nainamo. When the driver called out its name, she sat up and smoothed her hair. She wondered if Kevin would climb aboard, and sure enough, he did.

"Annette!" he said, after he had handed over his ticket and hurried down the aisle to sit beside her. "How are you? How was your holiday?"

"It was fine," she said. "I'm glad you're on this bus, Kevin. I was hoping you'd be here."

"I was hoping *you'd* be here," he said. "You don't even know it, but you had a big effect on my vacation."

"Me? How?"

"It was our conversation about black rocks. Remember? That really got me thinking, about what *my* small black rocks were. I realized my nervousness was one. Not knowing what to do with my hands. Not knowing where to look when I talk to people. I'm okay in a play, because I can pretend to be somebody else. But when I have to be just me, I get nervous that just me isn't enough. So, I smoke. It's a dumb habit, smells bad, makes a mess, is lousy for your health. So, I stopped. I got my family to help me, and I just stopped. I haven't had a cigarette since we talked that day on the bus. Can you imagine? I wanted to write and tell you, but I didn't have your address and the whole school was shut down. Everybody from the headmaster to the janitors was off for the break, stuffing themselves with plum puddings and Christmas goose. So, I had to wait till now to tell you."

Annette tried to imagine what it would be like, to stop doing something you enjoyed and were used to doing.

130

How hard it would be to resist. How persistent you would have to be.

"Tell me what it was like," she said, "and then I'll tell you about my holiday. I did some important things, too."